# CARMELLO

Also by Rahsaan Ali

*Selfish Intentions*

# CARMELLO

*Rahsaan Ali*

www.urbanbooks.net

Urban Books
1199 Straight Path
West Babylon, NY 11704

ISBN-13: 978-1-60162-057-6
ISBN-10: 1-60162-057-8


First Printing July 2008
Printed in the United States of America

10  9  8  7  6  5  4  3  2  1

*This is a work of fiction. Any references or similarities to actual events, real people, living, or dead, or to real locales are intended to give the novel a sense of reality. Any similarity in other names, characters, places, and incidents is entirely coincidental.*

Submit Wholesale Orders to:
Kensington Publishing Corp.
C/O Penguin Group (USA) Inc.
Attention: Order Processing
405 Murray Hill Parkway
East Rutherford, NJ 07073-2316
Phone: 1-800-526-0275
Fax: 1-800-227-9604

# ACKNOWLEDGMENTS

Wow. It is only through the grace of God, that I've been able to return and do this again. It was by no means an easy road. But I won't waste your time with my troubles. I'd like to thank all the readers who kept my first book, *Nasty*, on the Essence.com list four consecutive months in a row. A big shout out to Felicia Hurst and Winston Chapman of Black Pearl Books for teaching me the game. CHECKMATE! My publicist Dawnny. My editor Thea Cain. Great Work! Thank you for tolerating those late night disputes. In the end I don't know what I'd have done without you. My big sis, Brenda Hampton. They thought they were so slick, didn't they? LOL. Tangelika Bolen. Make'em feel the sensation when that book drop, baby. We're waiting on you next. My other sis, Crystal Perkins-Stell. Carl Weber. Roy Glenn. Mark Anthony. The mighty Poe. Dejon. Natasha. Courtney. Katrina. Cat Melvin. Charles Chatmon. Thanks for the interview. St. Clair Reide II. My sister. Alisha Rivers. George Eric Leonard. Alvin. Bobby. Chris. Thanks for all the help. Grandma Wilson and James. Daddy. Mommy. Tanya. Monie. Damian. Jonelle. James barber shop. My barbers Norman & Duane. Larry. Reggie from CBC in Wyandanch, NY. Grace Dyer and Rudy. The Reides in Cambria Heights and Elmont. San Antonio Rich. Steven Andrew Roache. Nick Etkins. Urban Knowledge Bookstore. My North Cakalaki fam. Durham! Davina the Diva. (California Love, ma.)

Aaliyah in West V.A. 204th and Linden. Wyandanch. Robert Thigpin Jr. GEO a.k.a Francis Black. Aubrey

McCoy. Denny. All the people who purchased my book while I was hustling between Strong Island and Queens. Long live Jamaica Avenue. My first home. And last but not least, all the urban-lit authors.

# CHAPTER ONE

## *Carmello*

"Sorry I'm late, y'all," China said entering the family room. Caine and I had been waiting well over an hour on her late ass. Women. You know how it is.

"So, what's up? Did I miss anything?" she asked.

I looked over towards Caine.

"I'ma be straight up," he began. "The cheddar is really beginning to look mad suspect and I don't like it. I want to get into the game for real. Niggas is making money hand over foot and here we are almost broke. I say we put the rest of our money together and take this whole fucking city over. Make shit the way it used to be. Smell me?"

China and I began laughing.

"The fuck is so funny?" he asked.

"You, nigga," I answered. "Take over the city? This ain't the movies, Caine. What we need to do is invest the rest of our money into a lucrative business or something like that."

"Oh yeah? A business, huh? Business like what? A resort in Cancun?" He coldly remarked.

Dead silence fell across the room. Once again Caine's illogical pattern of thinking and big mouth struck nerves.

"You're so stupid," said China, sucking her teeth.

China momentarily wept after Caine's insensitive remark.

"You a real asshole, Caine," I said. "Do you ever think about shit before you say it?"

"Muthafucka. We supposed to be doing this shit anyway. It's who we are; what Mommy and Daddy raised us to be. We were born to do this hustler shit, my nigz. We didn't invent the game, but we damn sure gotta play it. If you not going to do it for yourself, then do it for us. Do it for mommy and daddy. Play time is over. Time to take back what's rightfully ours. Avenge Mommy and Daddy's death. I just know that that slimy, fake ass, Tony Montana muthafucka had something to do with that shit. If not him, one of them dicks out there know who did it." China lifted her head and looked in my direction.

"Much as I hate to admit it, he's right, Mello. Somebody out there knows who killed Mommy and Daddy. That money in the streets belongs to us. I want what's mine. I want the muthafuckas to know we taking it for Mommy and Daddy," she concluded.

Nodding in agreement I leaned back in my new black leather designer Steve Harvey swivel chair and stared at my siblings—the siblings who once looked up to me for direction were now calling upon me to once again return to the streets of fire.

"Mello?" China said, awaiting my verbal surrender to the madness.

"Majority rules, Mello," Caine said smiling. "In your heart you know I'm right. You know I'm right. So, what's up?"

I stood up and looked out the bay window. A seagull swooped down towards the ocean, beak-spearing for fish entirely too close to the crest of the wave. Its watery hand grabbed the winged predator and pulled him under. It was almost like a sign. As if God was warning me of things to come. After a minute or so of not seeing his reemergence, I turned to my siblings. I couldn't let them go into this alone. No matter what the outcome, they were my responsibility.

"I'm in," I said, surrendering reluctantly.

# CHAPTER TWO

## *Carmello (One month later)*

Today was the day we were to reunite with Santiago to discuss admission into what was guaranteed to be a wild ride. But not before revisiting our parents' gravesite in Staten Island. We hadn't been here since the burial. I briefly visualized myself looking up from my own coffin at my grieving wolves, mourning for their slaughtered brother by the street poachers. Our decision to enter the game was one we knew would ultimately result in our early demise. One way in. One way out. That's why my Moms and Pops were dead. One thing was for certain, somebody was going to pay with their life. We came here today to kiss our parents' headstones and pray that their souls were still resting in the heaven that good ol' Mister Charlie promised us. We walked up to the headstones with our arms around one another for support. I took one more step forward and knelt down. Placing one hand on the stones, I inhaled deeply.

"Hi, Mommy. Hi, Daddy. It's me, Carmello. Caine and China are here too."

Forcing my tears back I continued.

"We're here to let you know we'll be joining y'all soon. We're going to find them muthafuckas that did this, hear? A lot of niggas is gonna end up real dead, real soon. That's my word."

I turned around to see if Caine was ready with the knife. We all stood over their graves and cut our left hand, letting our blood leak on the top and face of the eternal block of granite.

"We're on our own now, y'all. From here on out we are wolves," I proclaimed.

"Yeah, nigga! Yeah!" Caine sinisterly shouted, as the darkening clouds overhead bought down buckets of rain. It fell upon us as if Jesus himself was crying for our souls, which I deliberately condemned within the confines of the after hours spot called the "Devil's Cesspool." That day we said good-bye to each other for the last time. Our next stop was to meet with Santiago Decosta. He was the key to these vast and savage streets inhabited by those malicious gorillas in the mist that engaged in warfare. They were heartless, relentless, shameless money getters, who'd stop at nothing to keep their rims glimmering and their trigger finger itching.

We entered his loft in Soho, Manhattan. After being thoroughly searched by two machine-gunned guards, we entered the living room. Santiago was watching a video surveillance tape from one of his many warehouses throughout the states, on his sixty-inch flat-screen TV. What appeared to be his right hand man Carlos and his henchmen were force feeding dog shit on a wooden spoon to some crack-head-ass nigga. He squirmed back and forth on the wooden fold-up chair, tied at the wrists and ankles. Carlos pissed in the man's face, as he stood with his dick out.

"I'll be with you in one second, Mello," Santiago said, momentarily turning his attention away from the TV. "This is my favorite part," he added, turning back to his sick, twisted idea of entertainment. He snapped his finger for one of his many illegal immigrant hit-men to light his cigar.

"This is your last chance," Carlos promised the victim. With a mouthful of human feces and piss dripping down his face, the prisoner tried to stand and lunge at Carlos, only to fall flat on his face. His men began to stomp him. Carlos stripped a brown extension cord off its insulation and plugged it in. The exposed copper wires sparked as he touched the ends together. He walked over to the man and kneeled by his side.

"That was very, very stupid, my friend," he said pushing the wires up the man's running nose. His body jumped and twisted, while the men on the video laughed and threw water on him. Santiago laughed a laugh so unremorseful I began reevaluating our decision to reenter this madness. After his idea of family entertainment, he ordered his maid to bring out some wine. She wore the traditional black and white get up.

"Sooooooooo, Mello? What can I do for you? Oh excuse me, where are my manners?" he asked staring at China. "Little China, you look so different. So mature. You've become a beautiful young woman. Very lovely." He smiled with one leg crossed over the other. China bashfully smiled. She'd always had a soft spot for Spanish men.

"Caine, my main man. How's it going?" he asked.

"I'm a'ight, man. How you?"

"Living large in this great country, friend. I see you still have that tiger in you. You better be careful or one day that tiger will turn on you and bite your ass. So, what is it, Mello? Need money? Anything you want just ask." Before I could get a word in edgewise, dumb-ass Caine shot his bullet.

"We want the streets back again."

Santiago laughed along with his cronies, as he snorted a small mound of coke off a pocket mirror on the table. He rubbed his nose then sneezed.

"The streets back? How do you request something back you never had?"

"Our parents had it so now we want it."

Santiago continued his stroll down Laughter Avenue. "Ay, Mello, where you find this guy, huh? You come here making demands in my home?"

I quickly intervened, as the tempers began to flare up from both sides. Santiago and I both knew Caine could whip his ass, but Santiago's guns were a lot stronger. "He didn't mean nothing by it. Shit is real rough, man," I said, staring at Caine uneasily.

"Your parents were very wealthy people. Why come back into the game after all this time? Why not live off the inheritance?"

"Why? Why? Why? Who is you? The F.B.I. or something?" Caine asked.

"Shut up, Caine," I said. "Listen, Santiago. We want in. Our parents are dead and we don't have shit to show for it." Santiago sank deeper into his velvet couch and lit a Cuban cigar.

"You know, Carmello, I've always liked you. Weren't you in school or something like that? What happened with that?"

"No disrespect, Mister Decosta," China interrupted, "but that is hardly the issue at hand."

"Then tell me what the issue is exactly," he asked, inhaling the cigar so hard, that the orange glow reflected on the rims of his glasses.

"We want to begin where our parents left off," I added.

"And you're sure of this? Because once you're in, you're in."

"We're sure," we simultaneously responded.

"I like you bambinos. If it'd been anyone else, they'd be denied. But your parents were good people. I feel I owe your father a great deal of debt. So I'll grant you the streets in Queens. I just have to make a call. Miguel?" He called to his cousin from the back room. "Bring me the phone."

As Miguel retrieved the phone, Santiago reached for a folder on his desk and opened it. He had us pass it around to one another. Inside of it was a picture of Sunshine, a baller from Patterson, New Jersey who, in a year's time, managed to sew Baisley Housing Projects up with the assistance and intimidating tactics of his V.A. clique. He was interfering with Santiago's paper big time. He'd warned him on numerous occasions to vacate the premises but in the game called life, there is always bound to be trouble. It was all about chances, numbers, colors, and bubbles; trying to stay one step ahead of the next man, so you could be the first one home.

"We are all familiar with the saying, 'Nothing in this world comes for free,' yes?" he asked, outing his cigar in a marble ashtray shaped like the country of Cuba. "This is what it will cost you to join my family. I want him dead. I want all those roaches that hang in my building to know I called the order. I want this done by 6 AM. If you think you cannot carry out this task, you may walk away without tarnishing your father's good name and your own reputation. I do believe this meeting is adjourned."

"I believe it is, Santiago," I said.

"If any policia become involved because of foolish, unscripted action, you will surely join your much loved parents. Comprende?"

# CHAPTER THREE

## *Carmello*

Sunshine was a big dude weighing three hundred and seventy pounds, six-foot-five, with dark skin. He always wore a du-rag to match his outfits, and on any given Friday night you could catch him, along with all the ballerz and gold-diggers, lined-up outside of the sports bar/comedy club, "Laugh Inn" on Springfield Boulevard. Nothing less than a Cadillac truck would be parked outside the place. Sometimes it'd get so crowded that the supermarket across the street had to rent out parking spaces.

I met Sunshine at a bike rally last summer in Durham, North Carolina. He was big time. Always flossing and running his fucking yap. Another one of them niggas feared because of his rep. Most recently he started walking outside with no form of protection because he thought he was that bad. This would be his very last mistake. Tonight my boy Cartel from South Jamaica was performing on the stage. This would be our alibi. Unlike the movie *Juice*, no police would be walking up on us with any questions, because we'd never be seen associating with him. Besides, he was already very well known by the beast as a mover and shaker, who had one foot in the grave anyway. As Caine, China, and I walked through the double glass doors, the short, dark-skinned rotund security guard patted us down. I tossed a five spot in his tip jar. I immediately peeped Sunshine at the bar buying the house out.

"Drinks for everybody!" he shouted. We all nodded at one another before separating. China sat at a table with a lone candle flickering side to side underneath the high ceiling fans. She ordered herself a White Russian. Caine slid up on a table of females with Friday night weaves, and I walked up on Sunshine.

"What's up, pimping?" I asked.

"My nigga, Mello-man-Ace. What's cracking, my dude?"

"You."

"Naw, nigga, you. Diamond earrings, Rolex watch. You back in the game, boy?"

"Not yet."

"I told you man. When you and your fam ready, we can make this happen. With your influence and my power? Shit! We can run this city."

"I'm good, B."

"Whatever. What you sipping?"

"Henny."

"Yo, yo, yo," he called to the half- Spanish, half-Korean waitress with zigzag parts in the middle of her head, and pig-tails touching her elbows.

"Let my nigga over here get some Henny." We sat back and kicked it for a minute, while I tried to feel him out and see what his plans were for the evening. The whole time, China, whom he never met before, continued catching his eye. Everything was going according to plan. The emcee for the night announced my boy, Nasty Mouth Cartel, an aspiring comedian from the hood. He slid onto the stage and into the spotlight swinging a white towel with one hand and carrying a drink in the other.

"Holla!" he yelled. "God-damn muthafuckas. God-damn, y'all looking good as shit. Everybody except for that ugly ass dude over there," he said pointing to a purple-complexioned man, with a pound of Crisco oil all over his face.

"You's about the shiniest, blackest, nigga I ever seen in my life. Nigga so black his shadow got a complex. Got the nerve to be wearing a yellow shirt. Looking like some ol' fucked up cheese burger with a burnt smile. Ya black muthafucka. He the only nigga in here who got a job at the movie theater as the dark. Ol' African looking ass. Probably be at home cloning green monkeys and shit."

"What the fuck is you laughing at?" he said to the excessively obese man pigging out on the twenty-five piece buffalo wing dinner with blue cheese.

"You hungry man? I bet that shit is like dessert to you. You just look like a nigga who sit around all day eating pig's feet and sweating hot sauce. You better never walk past a soul food shop by yourself. Somebody might drop your big ass in a pot of collard greens and we can all be the Evans' family out this muthafucka. Dyn-o-mite!"

"Oh Shit. Please tell me you not the wife?" he said to the anorexic-looking woman seated next to him. "You the wife? Y'all sitting next to each other looking like the number ten. If I drew the number two on your forehead, you'd look just like a pencil. Ol' City Wide Testing ass. Looking like the only bitch in New York City who can walk the streets with your shirt off and get shit on credit. Ol' Master Card shaped bitch and shit. Charge it!" he said portraying a swiping action with his hand.

"There's so much bullshit going on nowadays. Michael Jackson running around looking like, 'Behold A Pale Horse.' Getting little boys drunk at Never Land. Dangling his son out the window. I mean the boy is loose. Who in the fuck names they child Blanket? He on fucking drugs. Michael, them shits is fucking up your life. My brother got hooked on that crack shit and ain't never looked back. That shit will have you howling at the muthafucking moon. White crack-heads is the funniest, especially since we supposed to be the ones always strung out on something. A Klansman high on crack came up to me when I was in Georgia trying to sell me his sheets and a noose. When I told him I wasn't buying, he tried to sell me a slave. The slave sitting up there scratching and shit talking about 'Massa sick.' We sick? See that was the mentality of the slave back then," he laughed imitating a line from Malcolm X.

"Stay away from internet dating. People put up pictures that's not even them. Case in point? Met this bad ass chick on there and we took it to the phone. She sounded sexy as hell, so we decided to meet in person. The bitch came rolling in front of my house with one leg on a roller blade. She pulled a kickstand out her ankle and greeted me on a slant, and had the nerve to activate her skate alarm. The sex was off the chain, but I just couldn't get past the one leg over my shoulder thing."

"Peace and love, ya'll. That's my time," he said catching a standing ovation for his performance. The DJ put on R. Kelly's "Happy People" and everyone began stepping across the dance-floor in the name of love.

After Cartel's small crowd of fans dispersed, I walked over to him.

"Baby boy, you tore shit up in here tonight," I said.

"It's nothing, playa. Just trying to pay some bills and shit."

"I hear ya. What's good tonight?"

"I'm about to puff a bag of boom and take one of these trick ass hoes to the telly." As he continued to speak, my peripheral shifted back over to China and Sunshine. He was getting nice as hell drinking straight Henny. Even in the dimmed lighting, his spinning diamond earrings sparkled. He and China both stood up. It was 2 AM by now. Time definitely was on our side. They began to walk out and I gave Caine the signal. He almost missed it, due to the compromising position his hand was in as it slowly crept under a female's mini-skirt at the table for four. She chuckled and moved in closer. When I finally caught his attention, he sprang up.

"Where you going?" she asked him with attitude.

"Gimme ya number. I'll hit you up lata, momma," he answered. She could tell by the way he dressed and carried himself that he was about making and getting doe. Chantell was always in the face of a nigga with doe. She gave him her cell number and tried to kiss his lips.

"I don't know where ya lips been, baby" he said turning his face away.

"Fuck you then," Chantell said.

"We'll talk about that when I call." Her three home girls tried coaxing her into talking more shit, but if she knew Caine the way I did, she would have known not to try. The next playa approached and she kicked it with him. I waited half an hour before calling Caine. All the while Cartel and I was in the dressing room. He was blowing one down in a cipher with two other comedians.

"Yo, son, I got to bounce," I said looking at the time.

"A'ight, Mello. Good looks on coming through to support a nigga."

"No doubt."

As I exited the club, I tossed the security another five. I hopped into my blood-red drop-top Benz and peeled off to meet Caine at a motel near LaGuardia Airport.

# CHAPTER FOUR

## *China*

"So what's up, girl? You ready for Sunshine to light that booty up?" he asked me while unbuckling my belt. This nigga really thought he was the shit. He just knew he was going to smash something. His little ass dick was so small, it looked more like a clit. All I could see was hair. I wish Mello and Caine would hurry up and call. They said they'd be waiting in back of the motel. The phone rang once and that's when I sprang into action. I began massaging his dick until he laid down. His punk ass moaned and groaned, as I stroked it like a pro with my lubricated hand. Keri lotion if you're nasty. As he busted all over his blue denim jeans, I wiped the remainder of the jism (cum) on his chest. The shit turned him on.

"Damn girl, you look gooder than a muthafucka. Can Sunshine get some pussy now?" The motel door flew off its hinges, as Caine and Mello barged in guns cocked.

"Somebody say something about pussy?" Caine said smiling. Sunshine began pissing himself. I moved towards the bathroom to get the nine I'd placed under the sink earlier that day.

"Baby, don't run. Just give them what they want," Sunshine whimpered with his hands up. "Look y'all. I only got four g's on me right now. But back at the crib, I got a safe. There's three hundred thousand there." Caine walked right up on him and banged him in the eye with the butt of his shotgun. A geyser of blood shot five inches in the air. He screamed while clutching his eye.

"Shut the fuck up, bitch," I said pointing my nine. I dug it deep into his forehead leaving an indentation behind.

"If you want some pussy, nigga, you need look no further than your reflection in the mirror," Caine said.

"What's this all about, y'all? Mello? Is that you? C'mon man. Tell me what's going on?"

"Hit the lights, Caine," Mello said. "Santiago says hello nigga."

Caine hit the lights and pointed his .45 automatic at Sunshine's dick. The room exploded followed by an orange flash of light. He didn't die immediately, so me and Caine followed through with some more fire. He still clung to his bitch ass life, reaching for breath and blinking. We all looked at each other, then finished him off.

Caine dipped out first. Me and Carmello bounced in the Benz. He dropped me off at my brand new home in Massapequa, Long Island. It had three bedrooms, two and a half baths, a pool, indoor Jacuzzi, and a heated floor in the kitchen. Caine was back in Baisley, where all of his flossing could be appreciated. Mello stayed at the house in the Hamptons. We all needed to be in different places if this was going to work.

It was five in the morning when Mello dropped me off. He said he'd give me a call later. He really looked out for us. He was both my parents and I loved him for that. I'd die for him and he'd die for me and Caine. In a few hours we'd be on our way to set-tripping on these blocks. Queens would belong to us once Santiago gave the word. The craziest shit of all was I felt no remorse for snuffing the life out of that little bitch-ass Sunshine tonight. There was no turning back now. For Mommy and Daddy.

# CHAPTER FIVE

## *Caine*

Mello was always Mommy and Daddy's favorite. Ol' ass kissing muthafucka. He be like the negotiator. The diplomat and shit. Always the problem solver of everything. He think he know a whole fucking lot. I'ma tell ya somethin' right now though: he don't know about a lot of shit. When this whole thing is over with, I'll be taking care of this family. Fuck Santiago! I got a team of wolves on standby waiting for me to give the word. I mean here I am out here grinding in these streets every-day bombing on niggas, trying to keep this paper chase cracking and this nigga Mello wanna chill . . . go to school and shit. Man, fuck that shit! I'm ready to go out here and lay the murder game down on any and every-body who get in the way.

Me and Mello were only brothers by blood. My real dawg was my left hand man, Starks. Starks had been in and out of the penal system ever since he was nine. He caught his first body when he was twelve. He killed his father with his own gun for beating his sister into a coma. He served five years in juvie and was released into a group home. Even though he was two years younger than me, he was all thug. I had mad love for any nigga who could make a fool levitate. Feel me? Know what I'm getting at? He definitely would be the first nigga I put on when my fam laid down the blueprints.

Sometimes I felt just like that nigga from that flick *Paid In Full*. I loved the hustle. The adrenaline rush that I got every time I beat a nigga's ass was sick. Or, whenever I sold that white to a zombie. Know what I'm saying? It felt real good to be needed. That's why I stayed my ass in the hood. But now these niggas was acting like I never lived here before. That shit was about to change in a major way. The call came in from Mello. We met up at Santiago's place by 6 AM on the dot. After we were put through the search procedure, he walked out in a purple silk robe, white fluffy slippers and pair of prescription glasses on. He was reading the paper and smiling.

"My friends. I do believe we have business to discuss," he said, directing us to follow him into his office.

# CHAPTER SIX

## *Caine*

When word hit the street that Sunshine was in his pajamas forever, niggas lost they muthafucking mind. Every other night a nigga was either getting clapped, stuck-up, beat-down, or ran off, by enterprising promoters of this super heavyweight division. Santiago suggested I let the dealers bang it out with each other before I took control of the Baisley Projects. Me and Starks were cruising through the Baisley area bumping 50 Cent's "Wanksta." Baisley was mine. But in every hood there was always one nigga that, no matter how many warnings he was given, he still want to front like shit just ain't really real. His name was Monty and his dumb ass was pumping right out of the lobby of the building I was living in. Bitches was laughing and hugging all over him as he flamboyantly flashed rolled up hundred-dollar bills. Niggas from our own set was riding his dick like trained professionals. I wasn't even having that shit.

"Yo, son? That nigga Monty is playing you," Starks incited.

"Word. I'm about to set it on that nigga. Ain't nobody

supposed to be out here pumping but me. This my li'l city, nigga."

We circled the block once more before pulling up on the curb. The screeching tires alarmed few. They already knew what was about to go down. We jumped out the vehicle simultaneously, both wearing baggy denim shorts, white Christian Elijah sneakers, and wife beaters. The crowd cleared a path and Starks made his way towards Monty. He continued counting his money, like we wasn't them niggas to be worried about. Starks stood in his face.

"What, nigga?" Monty said pulling up his shirt exposing his gat. The crowd stepped back in anticipation of a counterattack. "We all can get this cheddar, Caine. You can't just come back to the hood trying to run this shit, muthafucka."

Starks rushed him before another word could escape his lips. He pulled his shirt over his head and began banging him with all sorts of combos. I walked on his side and ox'd him straight down his grill to his chest. Blood soaked through his white shirt. I then snatched his money off the ground and pocketed it. Starks stole all his work and threw it to the zombies. Monty screamed in agony as his face bled profusely leaving a trail of blood. He tried making it to his car, but Starks ran up on him again and snatched his keys. He tossed them across the parking lot into a rusted green garbage bin.

"Stay off the block, Monty. Next time you die where you stand, bitch," I warned.

One of Monty's men helped him into his whip, so he could get to a hospital. He needed emergency attention immediately with his ol' bitch ass. Five minutes later five-o appeared asking questions. Even with over thirty witnesses, no one saw anything. That's how it was supposed to be. No nigga from another hood could get his hustle on in another man's proximity. So when a fool had to be dealt with, eyes were to be blind and mouths shut or you could be permanently silenced for good. After the cops left, I schooled the homies real quick.

"If y'all niggas wanna keep making your money, y'all best to keep the competition out of here. If I ever see that shit again, I'm blasting on the first nigga closest to whoever ain't from here."

Starks retrieved Monty's gun from the lobby and we bounced. We went to link up with Chantell and her girls in a room at the Marriott Hotel.

# CHAPTER SEVEN

## *China*

Sasha was the only female I associated with. She was in school and held down her nine-to-five as a teller at Wachovia bank. She lived in Danbury, Connecticut. After graduating high school years ago, she got with this fake-wanna-be pimp nigga named Lu-Down. At one time he had her turning tricks. He was an older cat, probably in his late thirties, early forties. She lived with him in his house—that is, whenever he was home. He was just an all-around hustler.

In a year's time, Sasha's gorgeous model-like appearance morphed to that of a battered woman. The magnitude of stress she was going through dealing with his accusations of her cheating and using him, had taken its toll on her long ago, so today, I wanted to do something special for her. I called her up and invited her out for girls only day. I treated her to a facial, manicure, pedicure, and a new hairstyle. We went over to the grand opening of Christian Elijah, a new restaurant on Manhattan's Upper East Side.

"You must really be seeing that paper, China. You spending like a star."

"You're my sister, Sasha. This money means nothing to me."

"I just pray you know what you're doing. I don't want to lose my girl."

"Whatever plan God has for me will be what it is. I don't want to talk about me though. This is your day. What's good? Lu still a bastard?"

"I'm really about ready to leave his ass. He hit me again last night."

"What? Is that why you haven't taken off them shades all day?" Sasha removed her shades. A reddish shiner rested under her left eye.

"Shit, Sasha. What happened?"

"Same old story. He came in drunk and high again accusing me of sleeping with any and everybody. I kicked that man so hard in his nuts he coughed up his dick." We both shared a good long laugh.

"Seriously though, Sash, if you ever need a place to rest your head, my home is your home."

"Thanks, sis," she responded hugging me across the table.

I didn't feel like driving all the way back to Danbury, so I invited her over for the night. We copped some Hypnotiq and an ounce of dro on the way into my town. It was the first time she'd seen my new place since I moved in. We walked to the backyard where the Jacuzzi was located.

"Damn, China, this is real some fly shit. Where can I change at?"

"The guestroom is past the kitchen to the left. I have to use the phone. Make yourself at home, ma." I hadn't heard from Caine or Mello in two days. Caine never answered his cell. Mello was on his way out the door when he answered the phone. He had a meeting with Santiago and would holla when he got back. I fed my fish, then went to my room to change into my brand new bikini. My daily crunches had begun to pay off. I admired my slender size and toned stomach muscles in the full-length mirror inside the walk-in closet. After pulling my hair back into a ponytail I grabbed two champagne glasses from the kitchen and filled them with three ice cubes a piece. Sasha was already relaxing in the pool, deep in thought.

"You comfortable, bitch?" I asked smirking.

"This feels so good. The water is great. Get in." I turned on the double cassette/cd stereo set, which sat on the opaque glass patio table with the Gucci umbrella. Musiq's newest hit was playing on power 107.1. I stepped into the warm water and slid down into a sitting position. We began talking about all the changes in our lives since we'd grown apart. We were sipping the Hypnotiq like water on the hottest summer day ever recorded. The hydro smoke, and steam from the water, sedated my body and mind. I hadn't felt this relaxed since my first professional full-body massage.

"You alright, China?"

"I'm good," I answered swaying back and forth to the soulful sounds of the crooked-eyed crooner. Sasha poured herself another glass of the blue funk. She refilled my glass before reaching for the dro. She began moving closer to me.

"I think I do want to get away from Lu. Does your offer still stand?"

"You're my sister. Whenever you're ready, we can make it happen. I'll get Caine and Mello to help you move your stuff."

"I love you, China. Thank-you."

She kissed my cheek and hugged me tightly. I hugged

her back with my eyes closed taking in all the apprecia-
tion. She pulled back and pecked my lips. I was in shock
and couldn't bring myself to form the words of disap-
proval. Looking into my eyes, she began rubbing my
thighs. I sat there doing nothing but letting her have her
way. She parted my lips with her tongue. I stood up to
get away, but the hydro and alcohol weighed me down
along with my undeniable weakness for her actions. She
pulled me back down by my hand.

"What you doing, Sasha?"

"Shh, just let it happen. I won't hurt you."

"Uh-uh. I don't even get down like this, Sasha. Let go
of my hand." Before I could say another word, my top
was off and her hands were pinching my hardened nipples. She licked and plucked them while I held her head.
Then, the unexpected occurred. She pulled my bottoms
to the side and made my body lift outside of the water.
Trails of liquid lust floated in the water immediately
after. She wouldn't come up for anything. No matter
how much I moaned and pushed her away, she continued her climactic assault upon my mainframe. Up until
now, I'd never been with another woman. I was strictly
dickly, but she hit spots that no man ever struck a home-
run with on my base. We retired to the bedroom where
she tasted every hole and eased every ounce of tension
from my body. By morning, we awoke in each other's
arms fondling and kissing into the evening. Does that
make me lesbian?

# CHAPTER EIGHT

## *Carmello*

After getting off the phone with China, I waited on my deck for Carlos, Santiago's man. He wanted to meet with me about some changes. He told me to bring two days' worth of clothing. I packed his money under them. A white limousine pulled in front of my home and it was Carlos. He rolled down the back tinted window, smiling, with dark sunglasses and a short-sleeved button-down shirt on.

"Come, Mello. We have no time to waste. Did you bring the money?"

"Everything is inside the bag, Carlos." I didn't trust Carlos one bit. He was a killer with no remorse. His smile reminded me of The Cheshire Cat from *Alice In Wonderland*; it was wide and unmistakably evil. I don't even think Santiago trusted him. He always stayed strapped around him. Then again, he was like that with everyone. I stepped into the air-conditioned carriage relieved to get out from under the sun's torturous heatwave. Carlos poured himself a cognac drink inside a crystal glass.

"Mello, have a drink with me," he said, while pouring it as if I had no choice.

"What's this about, Carlos? Why does Santiago have you coming to get me? Why can't I take him the money like I always do?"

"Relax, Mello. You're acting nervous."

"Damn right. I'm working with killers. How am I supposed to act?"

"Act like you're not new to this. Your parents were killers, no? Drug-dealing killers at that. So what is the problem?"

"Don't talk about my fucking parents, coffee-bean boy. I'll fuck your mule riding ass up."

He laughed, tossing back the harsh drink. He placed the glass in the holder and patted my leg. "I'm not one of your petty little homeboy niggers in the street, Carmello. You ever threaten me again and you'll see your momma and poppy sooner than you expect. Capeesh?" He began laughing again before answering the car's ringing telephone.

"Hello? Santiago? Si, he is with me. We'll be there momentarily. Si, the money is all there. See you soon. Say Mello? Ever been to Columbia before?" he asked as we pulled onto a deserted airport strip.

"No. Why do you ask?"

"Because, friend, you're about to go." A charter plane rolled out with its propellers running. Santiago was in the backseat.

"I'm not getting on that shit, man," I said to Carlos.

"But you have no choice," he contested pulling out his gun. The driver walked around to the back door and opened it. With his gun also pointed at me, I was forced onto the plane. I sat in between Carlos and Santiago. They both put their arms around me, as the plane sped down the runway and up into the sky.

# CHAPTER NINE

## *Carmello*

What seemed like hours upon years actually was. I didn't even know what part of Columbia we were in, but where we landed looked extremely poor. A limousine with tinted windows picked us up from the landing site. After driving for hours, we arrived at the most humongous and extravagant home I'd ever seen. Fifteen luxury automobiles sat in front of the mini-mansion. Beautiful Columbian women pranced around in skin-tight skirts, some in just panties, walking around and splashing in the pool.

"You know what I love most about home, Mello? The fucking women," Santiago bragged, as a seventeen-year-old mami pecked his lips. "American women believe that their snatch defines who they are. They're dirty sluts with no class. Si, Mello?"

"Whatever, man, Santiago, why am I here?"

"Patience, mi amigo, patience. First we celebrate, then business we speak of."

A fat woman and three little girls ran out and hugged him. It was his wife and children, he explained to me. He was sending them money every week to enjoy the lifestyle of the rich and famous.

"Come, Mello. Let us go inside."

The interior of his domain made me realize just how big and serious this game really was. The house itself had to be worth at least $5 million American dollars. The living room had escalators which led to the second floor on either side. A cube-shaped television showed four separate screens on all four sides. It sat centered in the middle of the connecting authentic tiger-fur upholstery couches. An aquarium built into the wall stretched the length of one car of a New York City train. A collection of historical swords and guns sat in a glass casing with solid gold trimming. I wanted this, all of this, but not this way. Not by any means necessary. There was a large oil painting of an old general holding a sword in his hand. It was an eerie looking portrait. Santiago stepped beside me and silently prayed before making the cross sign with his hand.

"Friend of yours?" I asked.

"My grandfather. He is why I am the great man that I am today. He gave his life for his family in this game of greed. His family never went hungry, nor his sons. Nor I. It just keeps going and going until the last one is gone. My family shall never struggle as long as the Decosta name lives. I have an uncle and children to continue the lineage. Isn't that the American dream?"

"The American dream is bullshit, Santiago. What am I here for?" I was becoming very irate at this point. I didn't know whether I was here for business, or if it was my last day on earth.

"Let us take a ride in my boat. We can talk then. Mami," he called to his wife, "Mello and I are going out for a ride on the boat. Will you please cook something up before our return?" She kissed his cheek and ran to the kitchen.

"Damn, man. You got it like that?"

"You can have it like that too, Mello. But no talking in the house. I believe the F.B.I. and CIA may have gained access to my home. This entire place could be bugged. When I find the traitor, his tongue will be cut out and sent to his mother for Christmas. They're trying their best to tear down what has taken over seventy years to build. Death to the pigs," he defiantly stated, spitting on the floor.

We rode out to the middle of the ocean and threw down the anchor. Moments later, another boat met up with us and took us to a home in a desolate area off-shore. It belonged to Santiago's father, Miguel Decosta, the man who was in control of the whole operation. Without him, nothing went anywhere. He was a short, hairy, husky old man, stylishly dressed like the old Columbian cartel gangstas who you only saw in movies. Fifty men or more patrolled the outside of his home twenty-four hours a day. His house was not as modernly decorated as his son's, but his air of wealth proved he didn't need materialistic items to define his richness and power. He was a very feared man. His men searched San-tiago and I as we entered the home. We walked out to the back deck by the water which was also heavily guarded by his vicious killers for hire.

"Sit. Sit," Miguel said to me. "So, you are Carmello's junior?"

"That's me. Did you know my father?"

"Si, he was an honorable man. It is unfortunate you no longer have him in your life. You have my sympathy."

"I just want to find the people who killed them and get out of this game."

"Let's get to the reason why I've summoned you here. You, just like your father, have the ability to move product quickly. I admire that in a man. In the short time you've joined us, my revenue has increased forty percent. I'd like to offer you a permanent position in our family. I'll provide you and your siblings with anything you need."

"No disrespect, Mr. Decosta, but I'll have to decline your offer."

"I no understand. You say you're doing this until you find your parents' murderers? What does finding the killers have to do with you working for me?" He had me there. If we had not been spending our money so frivolously, I would've never gone back to this life. I did like making money. You couldn't make money busting your ass your whole life just to constantly be taxed by the government. Then to live off of a bullshit pension and social security? But something deep inside also told me that if I refused this offer, I wouldn't be going back home. My brother and sister needed me there with them. Fuck. What had I gotten us into?

"So what do I have to do?" I asked.

"Just keep doing what you've been doing. If you ever encounter any problems, inform Santiago and it will be resolved immediately. Never kill anyone yourself, I have hired men for that." Miguel spoke in their native tongue to his son and Santiago left the deck, returning minutes later holding two briefcases. Placing them both on the table, he flipped them open. They were full of money.

"Do you know how much money is in there?" Miguel asked.

"Naw."

"There is exactly $300,000 in there. They're beautiful together, no? Go ahead, Carmello Junior, take it. The money is yours to do as you please." I looked at all that money and just knew that I was really about to be in some bullshit now.

"So do we have a deal?" he asked, tearing a piece of bread from the seeded breadstick that sat in front of him on the table.

"Yeah man, but soon as I find them killers, I'm out."

"Carmello Junior, you're not seeing the big picture."

"What's the big picture?"

"Let me tell you a story, Carmello Junior. When I was a young man, I owned several race horses. There was a promising young man just about your age who used to be a jockey. I paid him a large sum of money for him to race one of my horses. After receiving the funds, he pulled out of the race and vanished."

"So what happened to him?"

"The next month he was found with his head decapitated in a box beside his five dead children and wife. Get the picture?" he asked, lighting a pipe full of Columbia's finest tobacco.

We arrived back at Santiago's home a little after nightfall. The aroma of foreign food raged in my nostrils. We followed the scent onto the deck where his wife and her friends were cooking chicken, pork, and beef in the brick oven. The salty ocean breeze gave mild shoves to the seagulls who cried ear-piercing shrieks of laughter, as the orange burning ball of fire began concealing itself behind the blue water's horizon.

"It is beautiful, ay?" Santiago asked.

"It's hot man. I'm really digging on it."

"You can have all of this if you put in the work, Carmello," he said waving his hand towards the ocean. "Be smart. Make your money count this time."

# CHAPTER TEN

## *Caine*

My dick was still hurting from last night. Chantell sucked the shit out of it. That's why I was still at her apartment this morning. She lived in a townhouse in Shirley, Long Island. She was a stripper handling her business for real. Everything she had in her apartment was a gift from some ol' freaky nigga she flashed or fucked. I was not going to be her next victim. She wasn't getting shit from me, but a mouthful of these chocolate nuts.

"Chantell, where the food at, ma?"

"It's almost ready, Caine, shit. You hungry or something?"

"Hell yeah. Hurry up wit your trick ass." My phone rang just as I began walking into the dining room. It was Starks. Monty had come back for revenge and sprayed the block. Two women were hit and four children dead. He spray-painted on my lobby door window "BITCH ASS NIGGA!" I wasn't rushing out there for that shit. Things happen. I was hungry and exhausted from animal sex. I was making money even when I was fucking.

That's why I had Starks. I could trust him to run shit for me when I needed him to.

Chantell's sexy ass had most definitely convinced me to shirk responsibility. Her cool-red silk panties combined with her warm body temperature awakened my lethargic cobra, as she wiggled her ass in between the small space in my lap. She fed me cheese toast with grits folded inside of it. On the side was beef bacon and waffles. She was one of those bitches whose family was from the south. She could jam in the kitchen and in the bed. Between bites of bacon and sips of orange juice, I found room to suck her Hershey Kiss-colored nipples. She grabbed the back of my head pushing her entire soft and warm luscious tit inside my mouth. My dick grew into mammoth proportion. Then the damn door bell rang.

"Chantell!" The angry male voice demanded. She jumped off my lap and closed her robe.

"Who that, Chantell?" I interrogated, reaching for the bat on the side of the silver refrigerator. She pulled back the purple curtain at the living room window to look on the porch. There was a little nigga with braids standing there mean-mugging her.

"Damn. That nigga is a pain," she said sucking her teeth.

I walked to the door in my boxers and opened it. This nigga was little as hell. He appeared to be in his late twenties.

"Who the fuck is you?" he asked.

"Larry, why are you here? I told you it was just one date," Chantell said standing behind me.

He crumped up his face and tried to barge his way in. I pushed him back.

"Yo. Hold up, son. You better bounce your little ass outta here before you get hurt," I warned him. He took a step back and tugged his pants at the waist.

"You know what, Caine? I'm not fighting over no bitch but I'ma see you later. Okay?" he said smiling.

"Nigga, beat nuts and bounce. Faggot ass mutha-fucka," I responded. He looked at us both long and hard before giving a wink of the eye. Walking away back-wards, he finally about-faced and sped off in his gold Beamer.

"Stupid ass muthafucka!" I yelled.

"Thank you, baby. Maybe he'll leave me alone now," Chantell said pushing the door closed.

"How that nigga know my name?"

"Everybody know who you are, boo. You that nigga."

"Yeah. You right. I am that nigga," I declared with con-fidence.

# CHAPTER ELEVEN

## *China*

It was the fourth of July. Carmello threw a party in commemoration of our parents' anniversary. It was a traditional black people spread. Ribs, chicken, macaroni and cheese, rice and peas, potato salad, and fruit salad. Liquor was everywhere. All the food was prepared and provided by Heart-Body-Soul catering. All of our peoples were there. Each of the nineteen tables sat eight people. We sat at the tail end of the table, closest to the patio's glass sliding doors. Mello had a look on his face that he only exposed when he was under stress. I knew something was wrong but he wasn't speaking. He just picked at his plate. Big mouth Caine broke the silence as usual.

"What's the matter, nigga?" he asked.

"I think I know who killed Mommy and Daddy." We both moved in closer.

"Who, nigga?" Caine asked.

"I'm not positive, but Mommy and Daddy may have jerked Santiago's pops on his doe and he had them killed."

"I knew it. See, I told you. So, what's the plan? We gonna get that muthafucka?" Caine asked.

"First off, Caine, let's be realistic. This was never about Mommy and Daddy. It was about you wanting to be some kind of rich thug. Satisfied yet?"

"Fuck you, Mello."

"Come on, y'all. Don't do this now," I begged. "We all had personal interest outside of them when we got into this."

"I didn't. I truly do want heads to roll," Mello said.

"So give up your half of the business to me and China and step, bitch," Caine said shrugging his shoulders.

"No. If I'm out, we're all out."

"I don't know, Mello. I'm feeling really comfortable right about now," I interjected.

"China, we've already lost focus on what we got in this for."

"See, Mello? You still the same selfish ass muthafucka. Here we are blessed with the opportunity to own this whole game, and you here bullshitting," Caine accused.

"I'm bullshitting? Me? Nigga, when that OPT kid split your fucking face open and you was leaking blood like a bitch, who'd you call?"

"Fuck all that, man. We need to be in this together. It's not just about making money. It's about us making money together. Letting these niggas know that if they cross the line, they are fucking gone. But you wanna go and act all bitch-made and shit," Caine continued beefing.

The party was jumping and everyone was oblivious to the argument jumping off.

"I'm acting bitch-made? Fool, I'm trying to save our lives while we still got them."

"Save our lives, huh? How you trying to save our lives? Huh, Mello? How the fuck is you trying to save

our lives? By keeping us broke? I'm not used to that.
You're not used to that, and neither is China. You gotta
come up with a better excuse than that, bruth."

"Caine, I'm sick of your shit. Y'all come on inside so I
can show y'all something."

We followed him into his bedroom where he kept a
safe under the closet floor. He pushed a button and the
four-foot steel box raised up on an electrical platform. He
punched in the combination on the digital keypad and
opened it. He pulled out two briefcases and tossed them
both on his bed. We looked at him.

"So? What the fuck is that?" Caine asked.

"Nigga, open the shit. It's unlocked."

"God damnnnnn, boy," Caine said after opening the
case. "Look like ol' Melly Mel been holding out on us,
Baby Sis." he said after whistling.

"What's up with that?" I asked.

"Let's just say I sold my soul to the devil to save us
all."

He went into detail about his trip to Colombia and the
meeting with Santiago's father. He also told us about the
offer, and lastly the threat. I sat at the edge of the bed
fuming while holding a stack of thousands.

"So basically these niggas kidnapped yo' ass and forced
you to sign a contract?" Caine asked sarcastically.

"If that's how you want to look at it, Caine."

"When did you become such a pussy, Mello? Did I
miss something, dawg?"

I guess Mello could no longer take Caine's verbal on-
slaught. He'd been letting it slide for years. The right
cross to Caine's chin sent him flying across the room into
the weight set. He shook it off and charged Mello. I tried
to get between them, but they were both way stronger than
me. I was shoved onto the floor. Fuck that though. Never
hit a black woman. I picked up a weight and started bang-

ing them both. Now we were all in the room fighting. Mello was getting angrier by the second. Caine was swinging wildly, until finally tripping over my foot. Mello jumped on his chest and pinned his arms down with his knees, then proceeded to pound his face in.

I jumped on his back trying my best to pull them apart. That's when Mello reached for the fifty-pound weight with me still on his back. He raised his arm backwards hitting me in the shoulder with the weight. He growled loudly with the weight over Caine's face, then slammed it down on the floor, two inches away from him. Exhausted, he rose to his feet and reached his hand out to pull Caine up. Caine slapped his hand away and pushed himself up. He stood nose to nose with Mello shedding a tear and breathing erratically.

"Fuck you, Mello. That's what's up," he yelled, knocking the money off the bed as he stormed out of the room.

Mello pulled me up and hugged me.

"I'm sorry," he apologized to me.

# CHAPTER TWELVE

## *Caine*

I went to the dealership with Starks to buy his new Hummer. He loved big trucks. He drove through the streets all day showing off the hot wheels. He had to make a run, so he dropped me at the rest. I gave all my wolves pounds as I stepped into the lobby, towards the elevator. I rode to the fifth floor. When the door opened, that little nigga Larry was pointing a .45 at me.

"Yeah. That's right, nigga. Oh shit!" he said. "Bring your punk ass on out of there."

How the fuck did this nigga catch me slipping? He forced me inside my own apartment. If he was trying to rob me, he was shit out of luck. I never kept anything in the rest.

"Lock the door, stupid. If you try any funny shit, I'll make your head a peep-hole."

This nigga was pussy. The gun probably wasn't even loaded, but I played along anyway.

"Sit your ass down, nigga."

I sat down only because he kept waving the gun like he was going to use it or something.

"You fucking Chantell, nigga?"

"Fucking her? You stupid? That bitch just sucks my dick," I laughed.

"Oh. That's different. I thought y'all was fucking or something."

In one swift motion he jabbed the head of the gun in my mouth. "Did she suck it good, funny guy?" he asked, as he twisted it in my mouth. "As long as I got this gun in your mouth, why don't you show me how she does it. How that steel taste, pretty boy? Don't suck it too hard. It might bust a nut." He chuckled finding humor in his own joke.

If I made it out of this alive, this bitch ass was dead. Them niggas outside, those punks in the lobby, that I called my wolves had problems. How they let this fool get by them?

"Because you so cute, pretty boy, I'ma let you breathe another day," he said, kissing my forehead. Backing away with the gun still focused on me, he turned to open the door.

"Oh yeah?" he said, as if he just remembered something vital. "Just in case you thought this wasn't loaded?" Blam! He let one off into my leg. "Stay the fuck away from Chantell," he warned, before running away. I dragged myself to the door, but passed out before I could open it.

I awoke surrounded by D.T.s in Mary Immaculate Hospital's emergency room. There were questions coming in from every angle. I wasn't saying shit. After two hours of stubbornness and revenge on my mind, they finally breezed. Starks and Chantell arrived an hour later.

"Shit, boy. You just Tupac for real, huh?" Starks raved. "Shot in the stomach, now the leg? What you doing, collecting wounds?"

"How y'all know I was here?"

"I went to your spot and niggas told me what happened. I slapped them niggas up for not being on point."

"Say, bitch? How that nigga Larry knew where I rest?" I asked Chantell.

"Nigga, you the one parading around like a celebrity."

"Bitch, you got my nigga set up?" Starks asked, slapping her.

"That's bullshit, Caine, and you know it," she argued defensively.

"I don't know shit, except his ass is gone."

Starks nodded in agreement. "When they releasing you?" asked Starks.

"Right now. It's only a flesh wound. Bitch nigga can't aim. Help me out this bed."

"Flesh wound? Then why niggas was like you was all passed the fuck out when you was on the stretcher?" Starks asked.

"I fainted," I answered laughing.

"Li'l ol' bitch," Starks laughed along with me.

# CHAPTER THIRTEEN

## *China*

"You know, Sash?" I began. "The other night was not cool. Not cool at all! That shit was way out of my character, and I think it's best if you don't move in," I explained while I drove her home. "That shit was just a little too wild for me. I hope you can understand." She turned to me and smiled as I pulled into her driveway.

"You're scared. You're scared because you might want to do it again."

"No, I'm scared that I might have to crack a bottle over your head if you ever in your muthafucking life pull some shit like that again," I replied.

"I'm sorry. We still cool?" she asked.

"Forever, bitch, forever."

She walked up the stairs to the opening of the door. Lu-Down waved as I shifted into reverse. As I drove off, I saw him drag Sasha in the house by her neck. I just shook my head. That's my homegirl and all, but I got much more serious shit to deal with. Caine just got shot last night. Mello wouldn't go to see him. I had a run to do, and couldn't make it there before he was released. I wish when Mello first said, "Let's just chill," we would have listened. Drugs and money were coming between us, and I just knew it was only going to get worse. I just knew it.

Every once in awhile I had to check up on the workers at one of the crack-houses on Murdock Boulevard in Queens. It was a well-known drug-infested area, where zombies actually owned their own homes. It surely wasn't a hood where you'd want to be collecting funds or selling dope without a piece of steel. Mello was already there at the yellow house standing on the porch talking on his cell. Damn. He really was beginning to look more and more like Daddy everyday. I parked my sterling silver five-star, rimmed, cream-white special edition Snoop Deville behind his 2006 Corvette with blue-tinted windows. Cashmere walked out the front door with a bottle of Syzurp in his left hand. As I approached the porch, he smiled.

"Looking good, China. Looking real good."

"Dun, we not here for all of that. Money is coming up short. What's going on?" Mello interrupted.

"Some new niggas from around the corner is cock blocking, yo."

"What niggas?"

"Some new cats from Florida. I don't know much about them, but they got some heavy artillery around there."

"So. Don't your peoples got artillery too?"

"Yeah, but these niggas is all busting at one time too, Mello. A beast just caught a hot one last week. You didn't hear about the shit? It was on the news all week."

"I thought that was y'all. Why am I just finding this out now, Cash? You jerking me around?"

"You know I'm real with mines. I can show you where one of them niggas is at right now, if you want."

"That's what I pay you for. You take care of the shit or everybody is out of a job," he said walking away.

"You heard anything about Caine since he got out the hospital?" he asked me, as we walked towards our whips.

"Caine is good. It was just a flesh wound. You should go see him, Mello."

"He's a big boy. The nigga is out of control. Fuck'im."

"We family, Mello. We need each other now, more than ever."

"Follow me," he said hopping in his V.

We went to our warehouse, which we leased in Westchester. That's where we kept the kilos of coke and all our money. It stayed locked away in an office with an electronic walk-in safe. Security cameras monitored the outside perimeter. We also kept nines, forty-fours, and AK-47s in a room by themselves, spread across a long table. On the paneled wall of the office, was a blown-up picture of our parents and us when we were younger. There was also a bar and kitchen. Mello poured us both a drink. I rolled an L and puffed one for self. Mello didn't smoke. I inhaled deeply and caught the mad head-rush. Mello used the money machine to count the week's intake, then handed me $50,000. After placing the other $345,000 in the safe, he sat down in the chair behind the desk.

"So what now, Mello? You just going to cut your brother off?"

"Caine cut himself off. He thinks he got this whole shit figured out."

"I admit that he can be a real dick-head at times, but we family, man." He lifted his brows at me questionably.

"Alright. He can be a dick-head most of the time."

He still gave me that look.

"Damn, Mello, all the time, okay? But we . . . you have to bring that nigga home. It's only us out here. The streets is watching."

"No, Santiago is watching. Do you understand how much trouble we're in, China? We may not even live long enough to find out who killed Mommy and Daddy. I think we are being set up."

"So, fuck it then. Let's just make money. Then in another year we can invest in some real estate in Florida and live lovely."

"Let me ask you a question, China. Was this ever really about Mommy and Daddy or was it more about you living out your diva fantasy?"

"Yo, fuck you, nigga. You been acting real nasty ever since you started making doe again. You know who you're beginning to sound like? Daddy. Remember how he used to shit on us sometimes when his money was cracking. He'd shit on us all, including Mommy. He'd disappear for weeks at a time with Uncle Todd."

"You're just like her," he retaliated. "Acting like you be doing big shit. When, on the contrary, all you really do is sit back and get paid."

"Bastard!" I said, slapping his face.

"The truth hurts, doesn't it?" he coldly asked, knocking back a shot of Christian Elijah. I slapped his face again.

"I'm not Caine, nigga. I'll fuck you up," I said, raising my hand again for another slap attack. Before my open hand could connect with his face, he caught it by the wrist and squeezed, hard!

"You crazy or something, girl?"

"Let me go," I yelled, snatching my wrist from his vice-like grip.

"Go on home," he demanded.

"Know what, Mello? I think Caine had the right idea. I'm through with you too."

"Go ahead then. See how long both of y'all last out there without me."

# CHAPTER FOURTEEN

## *Caine*

Even with that bullshit Chantell got me into earlier, her ass was still fly as hell. She was nursing a nigga back to health in a house me and Starks copped in Hempstead. Starks was rolling an L when me and Chantell came downstairs. Before she walked out the front door, I gave her five hundred dollars.

"What's this for?" she asked.

"Go shopping, ma. That's for nursing a nigga back into shape."

"No," she refused, handing the money back. "I'm not with you for your money. I have my own, thank you," she added, pecking my lips. I closed the door behind her as Starks passed me the L.

"You's a dumb nigga, yo," he said.

"What you talking about?"

"That bitch set you up, B. What? You that whipped, partna? Then you bring the bitch to the batcave too?"

"Baby boy, my mind be working on overtime, my nigga. Ain't no way in the world I'm going to believe her ass ain't have nothing to do with that shit. That's why I bought her here. See, I know Chantell love money. She used to set niggas up to have they shit robbed way back. I guess she back in business."

"So upon that factor, nigga, why in the fuck did you bring her ass here?" he yelled.

"Slow your roll, partna. That bitch is so stupid she gonna try and have us robbed. Just like she did in Baisley. I'ma have her come here Friday night. She gonna think it's just me here alone. That's probably when she'll have them niggas run up in here. When that happens, we just blast everybody, especially her hood-rat ass. Feel me?"

"I like that plan." Starks' cell-phone rang. "Hello? Oooh. What the deal, B? Yo, hold on? The reception in this house is booty. I'm stepping out for a minute. You can kill that L," he offered me.

When he walked back in, he was smiling.

"What nigga?" I asked.

"I found out where Monty is holed up at. Ready to make this happen?"

"Word," I said limping up the stairs to my room to get my gun.

# CHAPTER FIFTEEN

## *Carmello*

"Carmello, where is your brother with my money?" Santiago yelled through the phone. It had been three weeks since I'd spoken to Caine; two weeks since I'd heard from China. I knew this shit was going to happen. Caine was fucking up. Damn it!

"Carmello. Are you there?"

"Yeah, Santiago. I'm here."

"Where is your brother? He's two weeks late."

"I don't know where he's at. I haven't seen Caine in three weeks."

"I trust there are no problems?"

"No. Just some family affairs is all."

"Make sure your brother gets this message. Have my money on Friday. Or you, Carmello, my friend, will be short one kin. Capeesh?"

"Capeesh."

I knew right then and there that I was going to kill this man. No matter what the outcome, Santiago always kept his word. I had to find Caine before Santiago did. If my peoples had never got in the game, we wouldn't be going through this. Why God? Why me? Why us?

I had moves to make. Cashmere had hit the hip and told me niggas was acting up again. I jetted out there in record time. He was sitting on the porch bleeding from the thigh. It stained his wife beater and his twenty-inch platinum Jesus piece.

"What happened?" I asked as the police began arriving along with the ambulance.

"They took everything, man," he said grimacing in pain.

"Get in the ambulance, Cash. You're a chump-ass nigga. You was supposed to be holding down the spot. I don't want to see you back here when you get released."

"But—" he began, trying to change my mind.

"Get the fuck out of here. I'm saving your life. This isn't for you."

The police began swarming the house and that was my cue to bounce.

"It wasn't my fault, yo," Cashmere tried to explain. Deep inside I knew this couldn't be prevented. It would've happened sooner or later. Shit, he didn't realize me cutting him off just might have been the best gift anybody had ever given him. He had a chance to get out the game and do something constructive with his life. The only thing I'd be doing was making funeral arrangements. I drove around the corner to the house Cash had described to me last week. Niggas was selling crack right out in the open, like they had vendor licenses, with the police right around the corner. I made my call to Santiago. He said his men would have it taken care of in less than an hour.

I parked further down the street under the blown-out light post shadowed by extended branches with wide leaves. I slid down in my seat and waited. Exactly half an hour later, two black vans ran up on the sidewalk hitting whoever was in their way. Six masked men, dressed in all black, jumped from each van in the middle-class neighborhood and sprayed every nigga on the block. Then, they ran up in the darkened crack-house. Shortly after there was a sporadic barrage of lights and gunfire. I could see this skinny dude creeping out the basement window on the side of the house. I sped down the block and opened the passenger door.

"Get in," I yelled.

The skinny dude hopped in. I sped off in reverse, cutting a right at the corner, then shifted back into drive out of Murdock into Hollis. As he began talking I knew this was my Florida guy.

"You must be my guardian angel, mayne. Where you come from?" I remained quiet.

I drove until we arrived in Flatbush, Brooklyn where a McDonald's used to stand. Now, it was nothing more than a lot filled with bricks, old cement bags, and abandoned stolen cars with no tires, windshields or doors. The nigga was nervous. He was sweating like I was down with the narco. I turned the music up and pulled my gun from the side door. I cocked it back and pointed it in his face.

"I'm only asking once, B? So come correct. Who been robbing my house?"

The nigga was so fucking shook he couldn't even speak. Tears formed in his eyes.

"Naw. Don't cry now, nigga," I said unremorsefully. "You can't play the game and be a sore loser about it. If I was my brother, you'd be dead already, so talk! How old are you, lil' nigga? Seventeen or something."

Dude still wouldn't speak, so I shot him in the thigh. He cried out in agony and tried to get out the car. I grabbed him by the collar.

"Wait! Wait!" he yelled.

"That's for my nigga, Cash," I said. "Don't you scream again, nigga. Don't you dare scream. Hold that shit in. Last chance. Who been robbing my house? Who the fuck you work for?"

"This nigga in Florida named Todd. I work for a nigga named Todd. That's all I know," he snitched with his hands up.

Blam! Blam! Blam!

His body slumped over on me. I opened the door and pushed him out, then turned the volume up on Lloyd Banks' latest CD and headed home. Todd? Uncle Todd? Naw, that shit was just too coincidental.

# CHAPTER SIXTEEN

## *China*

I pulled into my garage, leaving the door open behind me. I had to run in and out. Night had just fallen and Sasha was throwing me a little party at the Holiday Inn off the Van Wyck Expressway. It would just be some of the girls and probably a male stripper, knowing her ass. As I hopped on the Southern State Parkway, I could swear I was being followed by a gold Impala. I first saw it on my way back from New Jerusalem, New Jersey. I was out visiting my homeboy Earl. By the time I reached my exit, the car wasn't behind me anymore. I drove around for a half an hour trying to find the place before eventually calling Sasha for the exact location.

After I pulled into the hotel's parking lot, the car I thought had been following me earlier blocked me from reversing. I reached for my hammer in the glove compartment. Two white boys dressed in t-shirts and blue jeans crept up on both sides of my car. The man at my side quickly drew his pistol.

"Turn the fucking car off, lady," he commanded.

"Who are you?" I asked gripping the gun, but concealing it between my legs. "Just do it!" The other dude
yelled on the passenger side. I pushed the button on my
remote ignition to turn the engine off.

"Now slowly, slowly open your door and drop the
piece." I hesitated not knowing who these busters were.
If they were five-o, they had nothing on me except a
measly gun-charge. My lawyer could make that case disappear just like the city did for the savages who murdered Amodou Diallo. Our judicial system is the fairest
system in the world. Nevertheless, to avoid becoming
another statistical victim of circumstance, I did as they
asked.

"Step out of the car, Miss," dude from the passenger
door commanded, while the other dude opened my door
with his gun aimed.

"My name is Detective Kilaneega. This is my partner
Detective Shudemall. Do you know why we stopped
you?"

"No, I don't, but I'm sure you'll tell me?"

"You're pretty smart," he remarked pulling a picture
from his pocket. "Does this man look familiar to you?"
he probed, shining his flashlight on the photo.

"No. I can't say that he does. Am I supposed to know
who he is?"

"You tell me. Does the name Rodney Hampton ring
any bells? A.k.a. Sunshine. He was found shot to death
six months ago in a motel near LaGuardia Airport."

Truthfully, I really had forgotten all about the son of a
bitch and I wasn't trying to remember him now.

"So, what that have to do with me?"

"We have over eight witnesses that claim they saw
you leaving a sports bar with him on the night he was
killed."

"I'm not saying shit without my lawyer present. That's all I have to say to you, Detective Kill a Nigga."
"That's Kilaneega. But if that's the way you want it, then that's the way it'll be. Mike, call it in. We got our suspect."

# CHAPTER SEVENTEEN

## *Caine*

I got Mello's message about Santiago's loot. Santiago could really eat a dick. I shut shit down in Baisley and was headed to V.A. with Starks to take care of bitch-ass Monty. He owned a club down there called Planet Rock. It had a first floor where all the dancing and drinking went on. The second floor was where the zombies could smoke and sniff until their hearts exploded if they wanted to.

After I did his ass in, I was coming back home for Larry and Chantell. Starks was always in and out of town on business. Sometimes for us, sometimes for himself. That's why the word didn't take long to get back to us on where good ol' Monty rested his head at. Now, I find out this nigga own property. He had to get got. We waited in that fucking parking-lot for ten hours before his ass finally walked out of there, with three duffle bags and a briefcase. He placed everything in the trunk of his black Benz. We'd rented a hoopty in Chantell's name with no questions asked. Starks must've threatened her into doing it.

Monty must've had a problem with trusting niggas, because no one was with him as he stepped into his ride. We followed him to his house. He parked in the driveway of his two-car garage where a burgundy 2005 Dodge Intrepid sat. He got out of the car and observed his surroundings before popping the trunk. He pulled the items from there and quickly skipped up the walkway to his front door. The dumb nigga never realized that we had followed him home. He looked around once more before entering the house.

"So how you wanna do this, nigga?" Starks asked.

"It don't matter to me, son. I just want to clap that bitch." Starks pulled out his phone and put it on speaker. It rang four times before Monty's voicemail picked up.

"Yeah, yeah. This be Monty. Right now I'm either whooping a nigga's ass or fucking your bitch. So leave a message and I'll get back to you."

I looked at Starks amazed, like, how in the fuck this nigga got his personal number?

"You got the nigga number too?"

"Connections, baby. Connections," he bragged sticking his phone back in his pocket. "Let's go, nigga."

He ran to the side window of the house, while I stood on the other side. The sun was just rising so we had to be quick. Looking through the window, we could see him walking up the stairs and his wifey walking down. They kissed and she headed towards what appeared to be the entrance to the kitchen. Starks tapped the window and she faced the mouth of his gun in surprised horror. I ran around to the front of the house. Starks climbed through the window and quietly ordered her to open the door. As soon as I walked in, I placed my finger to her lips. Starks held his gun to her head.

"You know what it is, hon," I whispered. "Call that bitch nigga on down if you like breathing."

"Montell?" she called, scared shitless.

"Damn, Stephanie, what?" he answered, walking down the steps in his briefs. "I worked all night. What you want?" He stopped dead in his tracks by the time he got to the middle of the stairs. Starks had the gun pointed at Stephanie's unborn child. I had mine pointed at him.

"Monty ol' boy. Fancy meeting you here. What's good, nigga?" I asked laughing. "I see your bitch got a baby on the way," I ridiculed, kissing her stomach.

"Yo. Y'all ain't got to do this, man. I got work and doe in the basement," he pleaded.

"Shut the fuck up, Monty. It's too late for that shit now, muthafucka. I done warned yo' dumb ass too many times about working my spot. Then you spray the block, *my block*?"

"Daddy, Daddy," his seven-year-old twin daughters cried, running down the stairs hugging him around the waist.

"You better shut them little bitches the fuck up," Starks threatened, grabbing Stephanie around her neck and pointing the gun at them.

"You'd kill innocent children?" Stephanie asked crying.

"Bitch! This is business. Ain't no love. Now where is the basement?" he yelled.

I let Monty and one of his daughters lead the way down into the basement, while I held the other at bay with my gun. Stephanie was held down behind us by Starks. I did feel bad that the bitch was pregnant, but shit happens. When we all got downstairs, her stomach began hurting. Starks pushed her onto the red leather couch. "Relax, bitch, this'll all be over in a minute."

Monty looked on in fear and rage.

"Nigga, sit your bitch-ass down. Y'all too," I said to the girls.

"It'll be alright, Tia and Tanya. Calm down," Stephanie said consoling the girls with tender embraces.

They all sat on the couch scrunched-up together shivering.

"Okay, so where it at?" I asked. He pointed at a black curtain. I pulled it back and there before us lay ten kilos of white, $280,000, and four police-issued Kevlar vests.

"Take the shit and bounce. Now we even. I swear I'm done in New York," Monty promised. Me and Starks both laughed.

"Fool, you ain't in no position to be shot-calling," I said.

"If you gonna kill me, then handle your business. But they ain't got shit to do with our beef."

"Please don't kill my daddy," Tia begged.

"Yo, nigga?" Starks began. "Take all that shit out to the car, man. Give me the keys to the Benz, Montell!" he laughed.

Monty pulled them from his pocket and slammed them down into Stark's palm. Starks tossed them to me. It took about forty-five minutes to transfer everything from the basement to where the Benz was. When I returned, Starks still had them held down just itching to drop some bodies.

"Know what, Monty ol' boy? Looks like this is the end of the line. Too bad. This bitch don't look half-bad," he said, nodding his head towards Stephanie. "I bet you suck a mean dick, don't you?" he asked stroking his hand through her long hair. "Oops, pardon me kids," he said covering his mouth. "Mommy never told y'all how she swallowed your other brothers and sisters? Let me show you how," he said unzipping his pants.

"No!" Stephanie cried.

"Yes!" he said, pulling his dick out.

"You'd make me do this in front of my children?"

"Yo, Starks, what you doing man? The kids," I said.

"Fuck those li'l bitches. Y'all hear me? Fuck y'all."

The twins cried and held Stephanie tighter.

"Come on, Starks," Monty pleaded once more.

"I know. I know." he chuckled. "Not in front of the kids, right? Alright. I got you."

Blam! Blam! Starks heartlessly let off two perfectly aimed shots into the two sisters' chests. Before the shock could kick in, Starks killed Monty, then Stephanie.

"You slow nigga. Let's go," He said callously, frowning at me.

We checked the window before running out the front door.

# CHAPTER EIGHTEEN

## *Carmello*

"You know, Carmello, when I first welcomed you and your siblings into my organization, I truly believed we'd be happy. But once again, it appears I've gone against my better judgment," Santiago began. I sat in his office with this week's money.

"Your brother is fucking up. He better be here some time today. Also, he doesn't have that building anymore. I've found a replacement for him. You'll be meeting him soon, possibly this evening. His name is Monty. He's from Virginia. Your brother may have crossed paths with him once or twice. What balls he had to sell his own shit in my spot. He'll gain respect quickly. Your brother can work the corner. By the way, just in case you didn't know, your sister was arrested last night. She's a suspect in the murder of that cockroach Sunshine. Her bail is thirty-thousand."

"I'll take care of it," I said.

"Oh, I already have. I had Carlos go to post the bail along with my very expensive lawyer. She should be here within the hour." I stared at Santiago with the fire of the devil in my eyes.

"Is there a problem, Carmello?"

"My sister better make it here safe or I'll kill you."

He laughed so long and hard he began choking. The front door opened and Carlos walked in with China behind him. I stood up and embraced her in my arms.

"How touching. The family reunion. All we're missing now is Caine," Santiago said. "Find your brother, Mello. Your sister can stay here with me until then. She'll be fine."

"China comes with me. Let's go, China," I said taking her by the hand.

"She stays!" Santiago said rising from behind his desk.

"You ain't shit, muthafucka!" China burst out. "You lucky I ain't got no gat or I'd blast your fucking head off."

Santiago sat down and leaned back in his chair clasping his hands together under his chin.

"Go," he said waving his hand. "You are *all* my property now. So don't even think of leaving the country because I will leave no stone unturned until I find you. I will have my men hunt you down and slaughter you like pigs. It's not about your brother, it's about loyalty. I continue doing favors for you and you want to run out on me. But you won't get very far. I'll see you next week, Mello."

# CHAPTER NINETEEN

## *Carmello*

"China, we have to find this dumb nigga," I said, as we hit up the comedy club where Cartel was performing. I figured, after all the drama, we could use a good laugh. Somehow no matter what he said, I just couldn't bring myself to crack a smile. Neither could China. We made an early exit and went to eat at a nearby McDonald's. We sat in the parking lot while we ate. She told me what went down with the beast. I told her what I had to do in Brook-Nam. It was so funny how one hasty decision had turned all our lives inside out. After dinner, I took her out to Sasha's house. She'd be safe there until I could get my head right and come up with a plan to get us out of this shit.

"I don't be needing no troubles around here," said Lu-Down. He stood in the hallway puffing a Black & Mild Cigar. I turned around and walked to him.

"You want me to kick your ass?" I asked him.

"You ain't kicking shit in my house."

I fucked him up something terrible. After I finished, I made him apologize to Sasha for all the times he hit her.

Then, I made him promise he wouldn't go after her when we were gone. Turning our attention towards the TV, another breaking news report came over the airwaves. An Asian woman reporter from Virginia stood in front of a home in a middle-class suburban neighborhood. In the background were four body-bags being carried out of the home. Two were bags for children. Police and detectives scurried in and out of the house dusting for prints. A drug-dealer, known only as Monty, a woman, and two children were murdered some time in the early hours of the morning. They concluded the horrific story by piecing together a possible connection between Sunshine's murder and this one. I stayed at Sasha's house that night with my sister. I wasn't letting her out of my sight.

# CHAPTER TWENTY

## *Caine*

"Nigga, you was supposed to be here an hour ago. The bitch on her way!" I yelled at Starks through the phone. I was waiting on Chantell's punk ass when the bell rang. I knew it was her. I buzzed her in with the intercom we had installed last week.

Shit! She walked into my room with her tits just poking. She jumped out of her black leather skirt and pulled my boxers down. My dick popped up like a spring.

"Is that your gun? Or is somebody just happy to see me?" she seductively joked. I heard the front door creak. I threw her off of me and grabbed the gun from under the pillow.

"Tell 'em to get up here or I'll blast you, bitch," I said pulling up my boxers.

"Caine. What you doing? You crazy? It's a surprise for you."

"Come up or I'll smoke this bitch!" I shouted at the top of my lungs with my gun pointed at her. A slender, but short bad-ass light-skinned bitch with silver cornrolls and blue lipstick, sensuously walked in my room wearing only electric-blue pumps. My phone rang.

"Yeah?" I answered now pointing the gun at them both.

"This Starks, yo. I been out here for about ten minutes now, man. I don't see shit. That bitch there yet?"

"No question," I smiled. Not even thinking why he didn't tell me she was here. He was supposed to be watching no matter who showed up. Oh well, two pieces of ass were here for your boy and I was about to make it happen.

"Hold me down, son, I'm about to handle this business."

"You gonna fuck me or shoot me, daddy?" asked Silver stepping out of her pumps. She and Chantell pulled my boxers down and pushed me to the bed with my gun still in-hand. Silver guided the gun inside her pussy. She wiggled it around inside of her moaning and groaning until she dripped gangsta fluid down my arm. She removed the gun from my hand and passed it off to Chantell. They both took turns sucking my dick and kissing each other. Silver then put me inside of her and rode the wild horse, while I gripped her titties. She must have just recently given birth because milk began squirting everywhere.

"Oh yeah, baby, spray that milk, bitch!" I yelled wildly, squeezing her nipples.

"Yeah, daddy. You like Silver's milk, gangsta?" She growled excitedly like a super-freak chained to a radiator at a Rick James party. She and Chantell began to lick my entire body. "I wanna taste your milk now, baby," Silver said. When I finally erupted, she wiped it all over her face and stomach. Chantell crawled over to her and began eating her, while riding me backwards.

"Oh shit! Oh shit! Ride that shit, bitch! You dirty-filthy-nasty-whores!" I yelled.

"Yeah, muthafucka. Push that big long shit in this hot ass!" Chantell screamed digging her nails into my thighs. Silver squatted over my face and I licked her love until she dropped next to me. Chantell jumped off the bed and grabbed the gun off the dresser before I could react. Silver got up wiping her mouth. "Call him," Chantell said, handing Silver the cordless phone and holding me down with my own piece.

"Yeah, We finished with him," Silver spoke into the phone smiling. "Yeah, it's cool. Come on up."

*Shit, where is Starks?* I couldn't believe I let this happen. Live by the pussy, die by the pussy. I didn't even get the chance to say good-bye to China or Mello. Fuck. How could I get caught slipping like this, with my pants down and everything? Worst of all, that little nigga Larry didn't get the chance to experience my revenge. Fuck it! If niggas were going to kill me, I wasn't going to cry. It was just my time. That's the name of the game, baby. I heard the front door open, and then footsteps followed. The silhouette of a slim shadow stood at the darkened entrance of the room. The bitches walked over to him.

"Well. Don't be a bitch about it. At least let me see your face before you murk me," I said angrily, trying to zero in on my soon-to-be killer.

"Shut your ass up, nigga. You ain't no real thug," Starks said clicking on the light.

I quickly sprang up in the bed, as Starks pulled out on me.

"This ain't funny Starks. Not funny at all."

"What's that Rakim said in that song? Nobody's smiling and this ain't no joke," he said cocking his gun. "So tell me now, Caine. Do it look like I'm being funny?"

"Why, dawg? We fam, yo. I'd give you anything you want."

"See, nigga? That's your problem. You think money

can buy you friends. You don't know what a friend is. You don't know what to do with all that money you got . . . but I do. So, you're going to tell me all the combinations to the safes, especially the one in Westchester."

Chantell walked over to Starks and kissed him. Good . . . I busted all in that bitch's mouth.

"So hold up? Y'all been in this together from the beginning?"

"Nigga, me and Starks been fucking for years. You would have known that if you wasn't such a self-centered jerk," Chantell said, scratching her pubic hair.

"So, nigga, give up the numbers," Starks said again.

"Fuck you! Shoot me, because I ain't telling you shit. I should have killed your trick-ass the minute you walked in here, bitch," I said to Chantell.

"You ain't got the heart to shoot paintballs, so just give up the combinations," she said.

"Fuck you!" I barked, spitting on her.

"Last chance," Starks warned raising the gun. He quickly spun around and shot Chantell in her stomach. I sprang into action, dick swinging and everything. In a flash, I jumped on Starks and we hit the floor. I grabbed my gun from Chantell's dead corpse. Silver ran to the closet, while me and Starks rolled around on the floor wrestling for our lives. With both our guns in hand, I managed to bite his thumb and he dropped his. I sat on his chest aiming the gun at his dome piece.

"I can't believe you was setting me up all along."

"This is the streets, nigga. Ain't nothing sacred no more. Ain't no loyalty. Niggas is hungry. Be a real man for once in your life, Caine. If you gonna bust me, then bust me. If not, give me the gun so I can clap you. I'll gladly take your share of the money and the connect."

Blam!

Without a second thought, I busted. I then used the remaining bullets to shoot through the closet. Silver's body fell out, and she died with her eyes open. I rushed into my sweats and a hoody, while collecting as much money as I could from the basement safe that he didn't know about. I tossed it all in a black duffle bag and ran out to my car. I had to get in contact with Mello. He'd know what to do.

# CHAPTER TWENTY-ONE

## *Carmello*

Within the past week, there had been all kinds of murder cases shown on the news. I just couldn't shake the feeling that Caine was smack-dab in the middle of it all. I couldn't worry about that now. I had to meet up with Carlos to pick up a shipment at the deserted hangar. When I got there, the place was crawling with federal agents. Carlos and the El Salvadorian pilot were lying on their stomachs in cuffs, guns aimed at them. I slowly pulled away and drove back to Sasha's house. The front door had been kicked in and was hanging off its hinges. I gripped my gun and cautiously crept inside. I smelled Lu's smelly-ass Black & Mild Cigar burning. I called his name, then Sasha's. There was no answer.

I opened the guestroom door and it looked as if there had been a struggle. I walked to the kitchen and saw the smoking cigar at the backdoor on the floor. As I approached, a strong pungent stench rustled my nose hairs. The horrific sight I bore witness to next churned my stomach. I knew it had to be the work of Santiago's men. Lu and Sasha were given Colombian neckties. Their throats were slit with their tongues pulled through it. Flies had already begun to congregate upon the profusely bleeding victims.

"China?" I yelled out. My cell rang immediately after the sighting.

"Hello?"

"Mello?" the familiar voice said.

"Caine?"

"Yeah. Look man. I'm in a lot of trouble. Where can we meet?"

"China is missing, Caine. I think Santiago has her."

"I'ma kill his ass. He better not lay a hand on her."

"He won't. There's not much time though. Carlos just got bagged with fourteen kilos at the hangar. I skated, so I'm not sure what happened after that. Meet me at the movie theater in Valley Stream. Not the black one, the white-boy one."

"The RKO?"

"That's the one."

"Got ya."

"Caine?"

"Yo?"

"Be safe."

# CHAPTER TWENTY-TWO

## *China*

"How do I know when you go before the judge, that you won't turncoat on my operations?" Santiago asked me, while I sat tied to a wooden chair.

"'Cause I ain't no snitch. I played the game and I lost. So whatever may come, comes," I calmly replied.

I wasn't afraid to die and he wasn't afraid to kill me either. I knew Mello would definitely touch this mule-riding-cocoa-bean-brewing son of a foreigner if he did. I just never thought it would end like this though. And on some real shit, I was scared.

"It sounds good princess, but I've already been fucked over by your wild brother. I've been hearing that he's quite the busy little beaver."

"I have no idea what you're talking about."

"Really? Your brother and his friend killed my new guy, his wife, and his two young daughters. How can you kill bambinos? Now, his friend is found dead along with two unidentified females in his house. I didn't even know he owned property. Your brother is a liability. He must go."

"Like my parents, right?"

"Little girl, I had nothing to do with what happened to them. You have my word on that. But that is besides the point. Caine is more trouble than he is worth. I am sorry it has to come to this, but you all knew the consequences of this game."

"I did. I'm ready for whatever."

"That's the spirit," he said kissing my forehead. I spit in his face and he back-slapped me. My lip hit my incisor tooth and began to bleed. Santiago pulled his handker-chief from his robe pocket and wiped the spit off his glasses. His cell-phone rang.

"Mello? Hey, mi amigo. As a matter of fact, I have her here with me right now. Yes. She is fine but she won't be if you call the policia. Have you reached your brother yet? No? That's too bad. Maybe we'll see him at the fu-neral. Start making the arrangements."

He then hung up.

"Wasted beauty," Santiago said aiming his gun at me.

# CHAPTER TWENTY-THREE

## *Carmello*

China's body was discovered in the marshland dumps of Far Rockaway, floating face-down in the filthy mosquito and leech-infested water—a swamp where abandoned cars had been put to rest ever since I was a shorty. I don't think for a minute that China's body was the first one to end up face down in the various swamp-like ditches. It wasn't long before the police began to question me about Caine. It looked as if every F.B.I. agent in the world was at my home. I had China's casket designed in pink, the color she would have wanted it. My home girl sang a rendition of Donny Hathaway's hit classic "Someday We'll All Be Free."

Over a hundred people showed up, wearing all pink. I wasn't trying to give my baby-sister no black suit affair. When I say there was not one dry eye in the house once the vocalist began singing, you better believe it.

*"Hang onto the world as it spins around,*
*Just don't let the spin get you down.*
*Things are moving fast,*

*Hold on tight and you will last.*
*Keep your self-respect, you're very bright,*
*Get yourself in gear,*
*Keep your stride.*
*Never mind your fears,*
*Brighter days will soon be here.*
*Take it from me, someday we'll all be free."*

I thought back to the day when China was first born and how happy Mother was. It was the day she became our baby girl. My throat locked up with hurt, as I thought back to her first steps as a toddler, and when I taught her how to ride a two-wheel bike and she kept grabbing onto my neck until we both fell on the ground.

*"Keep on walking tall, your head up high.*
*Lay your dreams right up to the sky.*
*Sing your greatest song,*
*And you'll keep, going, going, on.*
*Take it from me, someday day we'll all be free."*

A lot of people, after the services, commented on how good and peaceful China looked in her eternal rest. I begged to differ. She didn't look peaceful at all. She looked more like she wanted very badly to wake up, as if this was all just a bad dream. She wanted to see the morning light again, taste vanilla ice-cream, chill with her home girl, and go shopping. I don't think she was in peace at all, I think she was scared, cold, and alone. She was buried on top of our parents that same day and I haven't stopped crying since.

I promised myself that her murder would not be in vain.

# CHAPTER TWENTY-FOUR

## *Carmello*

I still couldn't believe all the commotion Caine had stirred up since he'd been gone. Every time he explained to me the steps he took in the recent murders he committed, I cringed. Two days after the funeral I was being sought by the F.B.I., after a warrant had been issued to raid home in connection with drug-trafficking. They didn't find any drugs though, but what they did find was punishable up to twenty-five years in prison. That money or the so-called gift Santiago's father gave me was all counterfeit. I'd never put it back in the secret compartment in the closet after Caine and I had the falling out. Now, it was all over the news: the police were labeling me a counterfeiter and putting my photo and information on blast.

Now everything was beginning to make sense. Santiago knew we'd be looking at him one day as the man who murdered our parents. He'd been playing us from the start. I had to get Caine out of the state. He'd been considering moving down to Miami ever since he vacationed there last summer. Whatever we were going to do, it had to be tonight. Santiago had his henchmen looking out for Caine. I was keeping him holed up at the warehouse in Westchester.

When I walked in, he was drinking, and smoking a cigarette.

"I want to see her before I leave," he said.

"That's not a good idea right now, Caine. You know that."

"It doesn't matter anymore, man. I'm fucked. I've got eight bodies on my hands. Nine, if they connect me to Sunshine. I'm a dead man either way. So, like I said, I want to see her."

After saying our final good-byes to yet another loved one, we began planning our escape route. We were never coming back to New York again. Instead of flying, we decided it would be safer to drive down to Miami. No doubt five-o would be looking for him to be copping a flight out of state. Before leaving, we removed all of the monies from the safe, along with whatever drugs were inside. Then, we set the warehouse on fire. Caine torched the Benz he had stolen from Monty's driveway and we were out. My phone rang as we drove down I-95. The caller ID displayed Santiago's number. I tossed the phone out the driver's-side window.

# CHAPTER TWENTY-FIVE

## *Carmello*

It's been a whole year since we've been down here. Caine decided to obtain his G.E.D., so he could attend college in the fall. It cost us a pretty penny to change our names, birth certificates, and social security numbers. Caine shaved his head bald, along with all of his facial hair. A nationwide manhunt was launched for us on account of his foolishness, but I think we're going to be just fine. I took a real-estate course and began selling property. We also opened a club named Fly Girl, where females could do their thing as long we received a forty-percent cut. We were finally out of the game for good. As long as we just chilled, everything would be cool. At least, that's what I'd hoped.

I was sitting behind my desk in my newly built office when the thickest female I'd ever seen strolled in through the single-glass door. Her ass jiggled with every step she took and her poom-poom shorts gripped her hips with possessive authority. Her white Reebok Classics, with the four-inch pumps, matched her white blouse that cut off right before her belly-button piercing. Her deep mahogany skin-tone mesmerized the eyes of those who dared to stare long enough without being rude. The air-conditioner rustled the top of her silky dark hair, as she passed under the occasionally leaky unit squeezed snugly into place over the entrance door. She placed a briefcase on my desk and sat in the chair for clients. Removing her designer shades, she crossed one leg over the other, and smiled.

"Mr. Jackson, I presume?" she asked.

"You assume right," I retorted, removing my reading glasses. "What can I do for you?"

"I'm looking for a home out here in a nice quiet neighborhood. Somewhere the neighbors aren't nosey. Got any place like that?"

"As a matter of fact, Miss—"

"Francis. Cynthia Francis," she answered extending her hand.

"What kind of money are you looking to spend?" I asked, gently shaking her soft hand.

"Money is no object. Just be sure the neighbors are quiet."

"I have homes in quiet neighborhoods, mostly old and retired white folk."

"That's perfect. Can I see a picture?"

"I'll do you one better. I can show you. I'm about to go on lunch anyway, so I'll swing you by there."

"That would be just fine."

We sat on the deck of the five-bedroom home. It had two and a half baths, an in-home grill, central air-conditioning, and was fully carpeted with a two-car garage. It seemed to suit her persona well—expensive, but elegant.

She approved of the home within minutes and exposed the contents of the briefcase to me. After some signatures and another tour of the home, I gave her the keys. She'd be moving in with her boyfriend next week.

She explained to me that he was a very busy man and was rarely ever home. I gave her my card in the event that she, or her boyfriend, had any questions regarding the house. After that, I went home to shower and waited for Caine to call from the club.

It was Friday night, the night when we made the most money. People from all parts of Florida came to party and mingle, with sex, drugs, and liquor on their minds. As I entered the club, Juvie's club banger "Slow Motion" kept the playas playing and the ladies playing with them. Alex, my head of security, stood at the door conversing with his underlings. He nodded his head, as I walked by him towards the elevator. Taking it to the second floor, I walked down the blue-carpeted hallway, into my office. Caine was putting away money in the safe, behind the picture of our parents. Security sat in an adjoining room watching the actions of the increasingly growing crowd downstairs. I poured myself a drink and sat down, closing the door to the security room.

"How's it going tonight?" I asked.

"It's going good nigga. I think this is the best night we ever had."

"Oh yeah. How good?"

"Like, buy another club, good."

"That's what's up. See, baby boy. I told you investing our money was going to be a smart move."

"What can I say, Mello? When you're right, you're right."

"Just think, yo, last year around this time, we were grimy and running for our lives; selling drugs like they were going out of style. You was wilding out and shit. Now, we got a second chance. We still have to look out for the police though, but this is lovely."

"Fuck the police, nigga. If them niggas ain't caught us yet, then they most likely gave up looking for us."

"Don't be stupid, Caine. You're wanted for murder. I'm an accomplice. We'll always be on the run."

"They'll never take me alive," he said boastfully, brandishing his brand new AR-15 from under the steel desk he was sitting behind.

My cell phone rang, just as I began to lecture him on his spending habits. It was Cynthia Francis. She said I'd dropped my wallet earlier at the house. She said she could bring it to me, or I could pick it up. Looking down at my watch, the time read 12:34 AM. I thought it was a little late to be picking up a wallet, but against my better judgment, I broke out to retrieve it anyway.

As I pulled up into the driveway, two gold Impalas, with tinted windows, sped off. I walked to the front door with my hand inside my waist gripping the steel tight in the event that a war was about to pop off. Cynthia opened the door before I could ring the bell. She was barefooted, wearing a lime-green bikini, holding two champagne glasses.

"Come on in," she offered smiling.

"I can't stay long. I'm just here for the wallet."

"Surely you can have one drink with me?"

"I don't think that's a good idea. Your man might get vexed."

"My man is just my man, not my owner."

"I'll pass."

"You got it, Smooth."

She walked over to the glass dining-room table and grabbed the black rawhide leather wallet and handed it to me.

"Everything is in there."

"I have no doubt in my mind. I'm about to bounce. I really appreciate the offer, but I don't need anymore headaches."

"Okay. Let's forget about the drinks. I'm lonely right

now and just need someone to talk to. I'm new in town and you're like the only person I know. Besides, you seem like a real nice guy. How about it?"

The worst scenario I figured that could happen was that her jealous man would walk through that door and just start shooting. I didn't need any police in my life right now, but she was attractive. So the ol' "try this apple" routine worked again. Damn you, Adam for setting the trend. I decided to accept her offer, but I wasn't going to chill at her place.

"You want to go somewhere?" I asked.

"What do you have in mind?"

Roc-a-fella's newest artist Kanye West was on stage performing his platinum hit single "All Fall Down" when we entered the club. An array of colorful panties and thongs lay at his feet. He began kicking them back into the crowd, as he jumped into a frenzy with his self-proclaimed, convulsive Jesus-Walks dance routine. Next, he performed what sent the crowd into a tongue-spewed fit of overwhelming religious emotion. The hip-hop crowd roared "Jesus Walks" and stomped their feet, as if the savior himself was tonight's master of ceremonies. I grabbed a bottle of Hypnotiq from behind the bar and led Cynthia towards the elevator to the VIP room. It was nothing big; just enough room for a sixty-four-inch plasma screen TV, six-foot fish tank for my fish, two catty-cornered cherry-red leather Christian Elijah couches, and a bathroom off to the side. I turned on the lights and air-conditioning, as she dropped her purse and flopped down on the couch. I poured the drinks and joined her.

"You got any movies?" she asked.

"Naw, I only watch the news on that piece."

"I feel you; how about some music?" I opened the bottom cabinet to the TV and pressed play on the CD player. Jigga's "Dirt Off Your Shoulder" played.

"Something just a little bit more relaxing please?" she chuckled.

Earth, Wind, and Fire was up next.

"Now I'm craving your body. Is this real, my temperature is rising. I don't want to feel, I'm in the wrong place to be real," I sang along.

"That's what I'm talking about," she smiled, slowly nodding her head. "So. I see you're the man."

"Not me, baby. I've just learned to invest wisely."

"You and me both. It's nice to see a brother finally doing something constructive with his life besides selling drugs."

"Who are you?" I asked immediately becoming suspicious.

"Huh?"

"Who sent you?"

"What are you talking about? Are you alright?" She was right. I was bugging out.

"My bad, baby, it's just that when you have a lot of money, niggas is always trying to take that."

"You scared me for a minute. I thought you was about to hop on my head," she nervously laughed.

"Naw. You're much too beautiful for that."

"Thank God I'm not ugly."

"So you wanted to talk. Let's talk. Where you from?"

"Memphis, Texas, New York, New Jersey, all over. I have to go where the money leads me."

"There's money out here now, huh?"

"There's money everywhere, boo. You just have to know where to find it."

"What exactly do you do again?"

"I'm an agent."

"A what?" I asked standing up.

"Let me explain. I set up all imports/exports guaranteeing delivery and prompt timing to their destinations.

All of my deliveries and incomings are always right on schedule. Know what I'm saying, Mr. Jackson?"

"Sounds interesting. How'd you get into a business like that?"

"Runs in the family. My father, God bless the dead, my uncle, even my brother. It's not an easy business, but it has its perks at times."

"I bet it does if you and your man can afford a place like the one you just copped. Tell me more about him."

"There's really not much to tell. He's an ol' school gentleman from New York, who works hard for his money. I met him back when I was on the stroll and he took me in. He did a bid on some ol' bullshit charge and came out richer than when he went in."

"Just like that, huh?"

"Just like that," she answered finishing her drink. She looked down at her watch. "Oh, baby. I'm sorry but I got's to get up out of here. My dude will be driving these streets like a crazy man if I'm not home when he gets there. He's going to love that house."

"I'm sure he will," I retorted rubbing my chin.

# CHAPTER TWENTY-SIX

## CAINE

Iloved my brother for getting me out the mix, but I just loved the game too much to leave it alone. No matter how much money you make, it's never enough when you making it legally. This kid named Dre from Texas was buying the bar, when I announced drinks were free for the rest of the night. Nobody can share my shine. That shut his ass right down. We got to talking and a very lucrative relationship was born. Dre was a little ass nigga, standing about five feet flat. He wore his hair in corn rolls and it seemed like his jewelry weighed more than he did.

We took a walk to the VIP room and talked serious business that night. The next day I copped my first five kilos of coke from him on consignment. The deal was that I would sell only to those inside the club, while he covered the outside whenever he was in town, which was every other Monday through Sunday. This time I'd be smarter with my decisions and investments. I'd throw all my money I made into a dummy account. After I was comfortable with the amount I made, I was bouncing to Switzerland on some cheese shit. I mean what the fuck goes on there? I'd be able to just kick back and milk the cow. God-damn, I'm a genius.

Me and Dre began hanging real tough. He reminded me of that bitch-nigga Starks, but dude was about getting money. He robbed niggas for real. He was an out-of-town nigga robbing niggas in they own hood. That's real. Dre took me to this Trick Daddy party, where big asses and trees was the theme all night long. This was my kind of thing right here. Bitches, money, and music. These cats from the south really knew how to get it on.

"You can run up in any one of these bitches you want dawg. They just want to fuck a nigga wit some doe," Dre schooled me.

"Shit, I'll fuck all these bitches."

"That's how I roll dawg. Bad bitches is all I know."

"You know any of these hoes?"

"I fucked most of them," he egotistically answered. "You see that thick bitch over there, dropping it like it's hot?"

"Where, nigga?" I asked looking past the ones in front of us.

"The one with no panties on." He pointed towards the light-skinned, well-proportioned girl, with the long brown hair tied into a ghetto pony-tail.

"Oh shit. I was trying to get some of her hooker-ass last month."

"She one of them stuck up ATL bitches and shit. I think her name is Neequa. Go 'head and kick it homie. She ain't giving none up though. She real stingy with it," he said.

"Naw, I'll pass."

I wasn't trying to push up on no fronting-ass bitch.

You know them chicks that always got to add a whole lot of other shit after they say no. The last thing a nigga like me needed, was to catch a charge for slapping some dumb-ass bitch with a slick mouth. Bad as my luck was, I damn sure didn't need to be slapping no bitch. What if she hit me back? Then I'd have to fuck her stupid ass up. Naw. Fuck that! I'm good.

After the party, me and Dre linked up with some of his fam from the game. We rented a hotel and partied with this next chick from Miami named Quanessa, and her homegirl Kherri. We had a pound of trees to puff and the night was still young. Eventually, my high began to take its toll, driving me down Horny Lane. I was sweating Quanessa, and stepped to her. We took the conversation to the hallway.

"So what's really good, ma?"

"You tell me," she answered, popping her chewing gum.

"I like that. All feisty and shit. Mark is the name."

"I know who you are. You're the nigga that be tricking on all these silly-ass hoes out here. Hope you be using protection?"

"You think I'd stick my dick in any of these southern bamma ass bitches without a condom? Not me."

"But you do still stick your dick in these southern bamma bitches, right?"

"Hell yeah. I'm a beast, baby."

"So what you want with me then? You wanna see if I'ma give you some southern comfort? You want me to suck your dick? Oh no, I got it. You wanna see me and my friend get it on in front of you and your little friends in there."

"Damn, baby, slow down," I said, laughing while covering my mouth and wiping tears from my eyes. "You wilding out. Is that the line you use to push niggas away?" I joked.

"Forget you," she said, punching my shoulder.

"Let's try this again. My name is Mark, baby. I think you are the finest thang I ever saw in my life. Can I call you sometime?"

# CHAPTER TWENTY-SEVEN

## *Santiago*

"Welcome home, Carlito," Santiago said, embracing his long time companion Carlos. After spending a year and a half in a federal penitentiary, he was finally home. They'd only spoken once during his long and grueling stretch. Carlos vowed that his first order of operation would be to kill Carmello for setting him up. He was away for far too long. It would have been longer, if not for the familia's long money and team of very skillful lawyers. He beat the charges, including drug-trafficking, intent to distribute, unlawful posession of an illegal substance, and resisting arrest. His time in Hitchcock Federal Penitentiary was spent mostly concocting the most vile methods to take care of Carmello. He'd do Caine just for the fuck of it. He and Santiago headed straight for John F. Kennedy Airport to catch a flight back home to Colombia.

After settling down in Santiago's home in Colombia, Carlos took a hot shower. The long awaited privacy of a jet streamed cleansing, gave him a hard-on like he'd never experienced in his life. He slept like a bear in the winter that struggled through three seasons of hunger, trials, tribulation, and self-preservation. By morning, it was back to business as usual.

"Welcome home, Carlos," Miguel said, as Carlos entered the kitchen of his son's casa. Carlos walked over to him and kissed his cheek.

"Gracias, Poppa. It is good to be home."

"There is much work to be done. Are you up to it?"

"If it consists of offing that *hombre*, Carmello set me up!" he yelled, banging his fist on the table. Santiago entered the room talking on the phone.

"Si. Si. Comprendo, señorita." Santiago hung up the phone.

"Carmello and Caine are in Florida. Did they really think they could evade me for long?"

"The woman has found them?" Miguel asked.

"Si, Poppa."

"Let's end this quickly before we have anymore setbacks."

"Wait, Poppa, there is one more order of business we must attend to. Carlito, we have a major problem," Santiago said staring at him.

"That is what I'm here for, *hermano*."

Miguel gave him a look that could only mean one thing, but Carlos mistook it as his ordinary grumpy look whenever there was a problem concerning his income.

"What is it?" Carlos nervously asked.

"Carlito, it has come to my attention that you've made some dealings with the policia."

"Me? Nunca. *Simpre* loyal to the end."

"You know me better than that old friend. My resources are impeccable. I never thought I'd see the day when you'd turn rata. Do yourself a favor. Be a man of honor and admit your faults," Santiago frowned.

"After all of this, you'd kill your only brother? I helped you build this," Carlos cried.

"What did you tell them?" Santiago demanded, grabbing him by the chin.

"Nada," he answered perspiring.

"Nada, nada, nada," Santiago sang. "Antonio pass me the recorder."

His guard passed him the recorder.

Miguel placed his gun on the table and sat up straight. More of Santiago's goons entered the room. Even his first cousin, Edurado. They were all wearing lavender sleeveless silk shirts, white slacks, and nameless white shoes that read "Made in Iraq" on the back heel. As the confession played, the faces of all the men turned into a vision of undeniable hate. He'd told everything he knew about his family and others.

"So you thought you were going to fuck me, eh? The man who took you out of the slums of Mexico?" He yelled spitting in his face. "Motherfucker, you will surely die today." Carlos dropped to his kness crying and begging for his life.

"How long, Carlos? How long have you been a rat motherfucker? Is there anymore rats running around in my organization? How much *queso* did they stuff you with to become *rata*. You better say something!" he yelled spitting down on Carlos's head. "Turn on the grill, Flaco."

Carlos continued sobbing on his knees, as Santiago's rage grew more and more intense by the second. Flames began rising out of the grill plates, and the iron glowing red.

"Is there a mole?" Santiago asked.

"I don't know," Carlos cried, with spit leaking from the corners of his mouth.

"Is there a mole!" Santiago screamed at the top of his lungs. He pulled Carlos to his feet. A hot thin stream of piss began to soak through the two-hundred-dollar lime silk pants that Carlos had on.

"There's this black bitch," Carlos breathed in and out frantically. "She's been with the F.B.I., watching our actions for the past six years now. They caught me one day doing a side pick-up." As he began to admit his faults of being involved in plain ol' snitchery, the anger of each and every man intensified. Santiago snapped his fingers and the goons picked Carlos up and slammed him on the flaming grill, holding him as he screamed in tormented agony. The smell of burning flesh brought back refreshing memories to Miguel. He smiled as he envisioned his father once burning traitors alive, as they screamed in disturbingly painful octaves. Their bodies slowly stiffenning, as their skin bubbled, boiled, and sizzled within the clutching grasp of the hellified flames. Santiago walked over to the screaming man as his men firmly held his face down on the iron plates.

"Diablo, esupir en tu alma."

"I'll see you in hell," Carlos faintly whispered in agony, before Santiago's banana clip exploded what was left of his head.

"Get the men together for a meeting," Santiago commanded Flaco.

"Do you see why now I never give you *solvente?*" Miguel challenged Santiago.

"I'll take care of it, poppa. Do not worry."

"You better. I will not lose all of this because of your stupidity."

"Poppa, it will be fine."

"How do you know it will be fine! You know nothing!"

"Poppa—"

"No, *Poppa*. You make things right, Santi, or you are no longer welcomed here. Go, now! Go back to America and make your family proud of you."

"Si, Poppa. I will," Santiago said, kissing his father's forehead.

# CHAPTER TWENTY-EIGHT

## *Carmello*

I knew me and Cynthia would eventually end up spending more and more time together. Every time her mystery man left town, we were together. I really enjoyed her conversation. She was smart and really knew her shit. We talked about our dreams and where we both wanted to be in the next five years or so. She had no siblings and her parents were killed in a fatal car crash when she was only nine. She also wanted to be married one day, just not to the dude she was with. It was about 7:00 PM when I got to her house. The door was open, so I walked in. She hurriedly stuffed something in her purse.

"Baby," she said, placing a CD in the player.

Changing Faces' "Fooling Around" began to dictate passionate crime in the process, as it crawled out the mesh-plated thirty-inch woofer speakers.

"I hope you're hungry. I cooked some dinner for us."

"It smells good. What you made?"

"Just a duck, miniature roasted red potatoes, chopped broccoli marinated in garlic butter sauce, and diced tomatoes on the side."

"Sounds good. You sure your man is out for the weekend?"

"Stop being so paranoid, boo. It's all good, poppa," she said placing the gourmet dishes on the center of the dining table.

"You are a very bold woman. I like that. You're not afraid to take risks."

"That's what life is all about, boo. Risks."

"You know, Cynthia. These past few months have been really enjoyable to me. I really feel you. You're on point with yours."

"You are my kind of man, Mr. Jackson. But I just can't shake the feeling that you have skeletons in your closet. You have a story in your eyes."

"The only thing in my eyes right now, is you."

"Please don't get it twisted, sir, I mingle. But my body only jingles for him."

"I can dig it."

"So you said you had a surprise for me later?" she said taking a bite of her potato.

"Yeah, you like Alicia Keys?"

"I love her."

"My brother booked her to perform tonight at the club. Would you like to come see her?"

"Of course I would, boo. You and your brother are really getting that cake. You sure y'all not slinging?" she joked.

"Never that, baby. We're just like you. Young, black, and investing wisely."

"But if you were, you would tell me, right? I wouldn't want to be caught up in the middle of some drug war."

"You tripping. Not me, but since you mention skeletons, why is it that I've never heard of you and dude's business?"

"It's actually not that complicated to answer. If you have anything delivered from a foreign country or sent something to a foreign country, you don't necessarily have to use our company name. More than likely it was run through us."

"And the name of that company again was?"

"Hodge Imports," she answered clearing her throat. "So tell me, Mr. Jackson? You ever delivered or recieved anything from a foreign country?"

"As a matter of fact, no," I responded, reminiscing about all the shipments of coke I'd picked up from the hangar for Santiago almost two years ago.

The blue spotlight encircled Alicia Keys and her black Steinway Grand Piano. She sat on her bench, overlooking the audience with gratitude before opening with her emotional ballad "Some People Want It All." Bouquets of white and red roses sat across the top of the piano. All the lovers and cheaters stood heart to heart, while me and Cynthia stood backstage witnessing the angelic songstress spread her wings and give her fans their money's worth. The song made me think of my family and every hustla I'd ever known or lost to the streets because of the game.

> *Some people live for the fortune.*
> *Some people live for the fame.*
> *Some people live for the power, yeah.*
> *Some people live just to play the game.*
> *Some people think physical things.*
> *Defines what's within.*
> *And I've been there before,*
> *But that's life's a bore,*
> *So full of the superficial.*
> *Some people want it all*
> *But I don't want nothing at all,*
> *If it ain't you baby.*
> *If I ain't got you baby.*

*Some people want diamond rings;*
*Some just want everything.*
*But everything means nothing,*
*If I ain't got you.*

The more Alicia got into the song, the harder she pounded the ivory keys of the piano. Her long braided hair glistened and sparkled under the bright blue spotlight. I thought more and more of the easy road I'd traveled to maintain this image, that painted a morbid portrait of my inevitable future working the graveyard shift in the cemetery with my family.

*Some people search for a fountain;*
*The promises forever young,*
*Some people need three dozen roses,*
*And that's the only way to prove you love them.*
*Hand me the world on a silver platter,*
*And what good would it be?*
*With no one to share, with no one who truly cares for*
    *me.*

Alicia jumped off the piano bench, knocking it over as she turned to face the audience. Tears streamed down her face as she looked on. Her hair blended in with her dark-blue pinstripped suit.

*Some people want it all,*
*But I don't want nothing at all,*
*If it ain't you baby.*
*If I ain't got you baby.*
*Some people want diamond rings,*
*Some people want everything,*
*But everything means nothing,*
*If I ain't got you.*

After her performance, the mega-superstar was whisked away by her manager and security to her next show in Tampa. Cynthia was impressed with meeting Alicia just before she left the building. She liked the idea that my brother and I could get Alicia to come here but didn't let it go to our heads. I liked that about her. After introducing Cynthia to Caine, they hit it off great. I guess she was astonished by his gangsta mannerisms. We all sat in the office talking the night away. The more Caine ran his yap, the more inquisitive she became.

"You look so familiar, Mark," Cynthia said, calling Caine by his assumed name.

"I get that a lot."

# CHAPTER TWENTY-NINE

## *Caine*

Once again the money was coming in just the way I liked to make it. Fast. I was selling so much coke out the club without Mello's knowledge, that Dre's main connect wanted to meet with me. He was to fly in from Texas with him the following week. In the meantime, I moved out the crib me and Mello shared and copped this butta-ass condo. The first thing I did was invite Quanessa's fine ass over. She loved my shit. Everything was top of the line. I bought a flat-screen TV wide enough to cover the living room wall. I had a refrigerator built into the kitchen wall, and a portrait of myself wearing a king's crown. It hung over the entrepreneur of the year award that me and my brother won last year. She liked what she saw and so did I.

"This is so very much you," she complimented, looking around.

"What that mean?"

"Oh nothing. Your place is cool. I like it."

"Thanks. I decorated it myself," I proudly stated.

"I know you did, boy."

"Always with the jokes."

"Always."

"So what do you do?" I asked as we sat on the designer Darryl Hos suede couch. Believe it. The cheddar ran long.

"I'm a nurse at Vincent Savon Hospital for Children."

"How is that? I mean dealing with the shorties ev'yday?"

"It's sad and rejuvenating at the same time. It's not a job I'd recommend to my daughter. It can be so heart-wrenching to see the amount of children coming in with gunshot wounds."

"How old is she?"

"Fourteen. Her name is Tyeesha."

"You look real good for someone who got a fourteen-year-old."

"Thank you," she giggled blushing.

"Oh, is that a laugh? Awww shit. She's laughing, y'all."

"You're alright, Mark. So being that I'm a guest in your home, what's for dinner? Something is smelling delicious."

"Yeah, that's my food. Pardon me, ma," I said walking to the kitchen. I returned with a plate of lasagna. I sat at the table and began eating, while she sat on the couch and watched. Her face began to frown.

"Baby, you gonna order out?" I asked.

"I see I'm going to have a job on my hands messing with you," she said.

After dinner we rode through the streets of Miami just talkin' about life and shit. She told me about her bitch-ass baby daddy. I told her about the bitches that tried to claim me as they baby's daddy. Just in one night, Ma had me more open than secret footage of the Bushes and Bin Ladin shaking hands. Her body was banging. She was also outspoken and made sure to bring it to my attention when I did or said something she didn't like. Nothing like the chickens in New York. They didn't care how you treated them; long as your doe was long, you were appreciated. I parked on the beach and we found ourselves sitting on a blanket in the sand. It was chilly that night, so I put my jacket around her shoulders. She leaned into my embrace.

"This is so serene, Mark. I love the ocean."

"It can be very peaceful at times," I said, looking at the full moon's light reflecting off the top of the liquid mirror.

"Why don't you have a girlfriend? I mean, you're a good looking man."

"Ain't no true ones out here, baby. Put your trust in somebody too fast and you will get ripped."

"Is that what you do? The ladies put their trust in you, then you break their hearts."

"It all depends. If you a money hungry ho, then you'll get treated like one."

"I'm only asking because I like you, Mark. You might meet my daughter one day and I don't need no man running in and out of my house. She already traveling down the road of trouble. I had to spend three hundred dollars for an abortion for her last month."

"That's crazy. Fourteen years ol'? Damn, ma."

"I cracked that ass when she first told me."

"And the baby's father?"

"She met him on the internet."

"I would've found that muthafucka and made him come out the pockets."

"That would have been great if she had told me who he was. The only thing she said was that he was much, much older."

"One of them R. Kelly niggas, huh?"

"Yeah. Sick bastards. Can't get no love from their own

age range, so they prey on children. Hurt children. Beat women. Just like that crazy white boy from New York. Joel Steinberg, you know? The guy who starved and abused his wife and illegally adopted daughter."

"Didn't he just get out?"

"Yep. The community doesn't want that nigga in their neighborhood either."

"If I was there, I wouldn't either."

"So, Mark? Now that you know a little about me, don't you think it's your turn to tell your story?"

"Now is not the best time, baby. But I'ma tell you when the time is right. All that matters right now is that I'm feeling you." She turned to me and kissed my cheek.

"How old are you exactly, Mark?"

"Twenty-two. A couple of weeks ago."

"Happy belated. Did you get everything you wanted for your birthday?"

"I'm not sure yet."

"Maybe I can rectify the situation," she said standing up and stripping, while running towards the oncoming waves.

"Come on in. The water is fine," she said, standing nude, waist-deep in the moonlit water.

# CHAPTER THIRTY

## *Carmello*

The choices we make will forever dictate the outcome of
   our lives.
Whether it's selling encyclopedias or smuggling nines.
Nobody really cares how many bodies fall in the street,
Nor the amount of overdoses and murders that occur
   within a week.
The war within myself is worse than the premeditated
   war in Afghanistan.
I've cut off more friends than decapitated heads in Iraq
   and Iran.
Sold more crack than shattered glass slipping out the
   butter-fingered children's grasps.
They all have holes in their hands sacrificed with their
   only chance.
All the families I've destroyed and bank accounts I've
   wiped out,
The tears I've collected from mourning mommas is so
   sad when they roll out.
Sporting diamond encrusted crosses, as if I had some
   kind of faith.

*Soon as I get home I wash the blood off my hands and
    face.*
*Uncertain if I'll be killed or crippled the next day,*
*My time is near I can feel it in my bones always.*
*Destined to burn in the rubble slaughtered by stones,*
*All for the love of money and sitting on chrome.*
*But karma comes back and my family was stole,*
*Kidnapped to the dimension of tortured souls.*
*Where payback is a muthafucka and viciously cold,*
*Black crows eternally peck away at your dome.*
*If I could turn back the hands of time I would've killed us
    all,*
*Instead of letting this life lead us all to the morgue.*
*This is for every little girl and boy.*
*You don't have to OD on drugs to die,*
*All you have to do is touch them,*
*And your life will be destroyed.*

"This is Carmello Jordan Denn. This is my last will and
testament. I've made a lot of money and have done many
bad things. In the event of my untimely demise, I'd like
to invest all assets and monies back into the drug rehabs
in New York City. I feel that Santiago is getting closer and
it will only be a matter of time before we bump heads
and he kills me, if you muthafuckas don't do it first. So, if
you find me before he does, suck nuts!"

I recorded my confession on a digital recorder, then
slid it in a manila envelope addressed to the Federal Bu-
reau of Investigations. I slid it in between my mattress
and put the recorder in my pocket. I'd be carrying that
from now on along with my pearl-handled .38 revolver.
Caine had something important to tell me at the club. I
took the thirty-five minute drive to the spot. It was really
jumping tonight. As a matter of fact, it had been like this

for the past few months. We were the only niggas having consistent celebrity performances every Saturday night. Ladies got in free after 1:00 AM, and could drink until they grew fins. But the crowd I'd been seeing lately wasn't adding up with the bank roll. This had Caine written all over it. Maybe what he wanted to talk about tonight had something to do with it.

He was in the VIP room with his new girl Quanessa. They were laughing and joking when I entered the room. He stood up smiling.

"Big bro, meet your future sister-in-law. Baby boy is getting married." I stood in shock before shaking off my trance. "Did ya hear me, nigga? I said we're getting married."

"Yeah. Congratulations, man," I said hugging them both. Quanessa was good peoples. I hoped he would treat her right. He had changed a lot since we came out here. For what it was worth, I did do something good after all. I saved my brother's life. Now he was about to start a new one. Thank you, God. The wedding was to be set for November 12th of this year. That was five months away. They'd only been dating for four. After the wedding Quanessa and her daughter would go live with Caine. I wonder if he ever was going to tell her who he really was.

# CHAPTER THIRTY-ONE

## *Carmello*

A month and a few weeks later, I threw Caine a bachelor party at our club. Everyone came out. Drinks were free for everyone. Caine was a child in candy land with all the females that were gyrating their asses on his groin. That's when it happened. One of the females got mad at Caine for being a little wild with her and he slapped her to the floor.

"This is my day, bitch. Now get up and shake your ass . . . but watch yourself." The rest of the night went smoothly after Ike Turner laid down the open hand game across shorty's grill. After shit began settling down, the crowd started chanting, "Speech. Speech."

Caine walked to the mic and wobbled as he held it.

"Speech! Speech! Speech!" he teased. "God bless. And thanks for coming out," he laughed, emulating the all too short farewells that Russell Simmons used to give before the ending of each show on the forever cherished, never forgotten *Def Comedy Jam*. They all laughed while throwing napkins and empty plastic cups at him. "Naw. Seriously, y'all. First off, I'd like to thank my brother for putting this whole thing together for a nigga. Know what I'm saying? A big shout out to the woman in my future, Quanessa, who is probably out with her girls being searched by male exotic dancers. It's all hood. Never in my life did I think I'd be taking such a huge step, but when it's right, it's right." They all cheered for their main man, as he ate it on up.

"You may kiss the bride," said the minister to my brother. They kissed long and passionately, holding on to one another as if their lives depended on it. The wedding cost Caine over forty thousand dollars. But what was a little money for a lifetime of happiness? I was the best man. I felt like a proud father standing next to him. Maybe things were going to be alright. Maybe the police would never find us. Maybe Santiago had given up on hunting us down. Cynthia's so-called man was out on business again, so she came with me as my date. She would've made a beautiful bride if we were the ones getting married. After the wedding, we had a huge reception in Caine's backyard. The hip-hop band, the Roots, supplied the music for the evening.

The couple planned to spend their honeymoon in Acapulco, Mexico. Her daughter was to stay with her sister in Tampa. That's when everything really started to go bad.

# CHAPTER THIRTY-TWO

## *Caine*

"I'm married, nigga," I said to myself in the bathroom mirror, as I finished rinsing the shaving cream off my face. Quanessa walked in behind me and wrapped her arms around my waist, resting her chin on my shoulder.

"How do you like your new wife?" she asked.

"I love my new wife," I answered patting my face dry with the white towel. We were getting ready to go to her mom's house for dinner. Mello was invited too. I guess he'd be bringing that bitch with him. There was something about her I didn't trust, but Mello wouldn't listen to shit I had to say. I had my own family to be concerned with now. So I never gave it another thought. What I was thinking about was telling Quanessa who I really was. But why spoil a good thing? If she was happy, then maybe I should just keep that on the low. She was about to take her shower, which meant she'd be about three hours. My intercom rang.

"Yeah?" I answered.

"Yo, dawg? It's Dre." I buzzed him up and met him in the hallway.

"Look at you, nigga. Looking whipped already," he teased.

"Yo, momma," I laughed.

"Yeah, dawg. Sorry I missed that shit but I had business to take care of."

"Ain't no thang, nigga. What's good with that connect though?"

"Dude supposed to be flying in tonight. Between me and you, I never met son myself. But that's the man who keeps us rich."

"Holla," I said slapping his hand.

"Oh yeah, dawg? I heard a lot of shit about wifey's daughter. Better sleep with the mac under the bed. She be going to all them Luke parties. Puffing stems. Fucking them ol' school ballers and shit."

"I don't give a fuck, nigga. She ain't my daughter. I married her momma."

"Nigga, you is cold-blooded."

"And I'm rich, bitch," I laughed.

"Mark!" Quanessa yelled. We both ran into the condo. She was standing on a chair looking nervous, scanning the floor.

"What!" I said.

"I just seen the biggest cockroach."

Ms. Baron, Quanessa's mother, was a very dark lady, with a gheri-curl relaxer in her hair. She stood about five-foot-two and weighed approximately three hundred and twenty-five pounds. Her hair was reddish-brown with hints of gray. Her over-exaggerated dimples and cigarette-yellow teeth, hands down, diminished any chance of this grotesque figure before me ever making it on a beauty scale of one to ten. She spoke so fast I thought a parachute would pop out of her fucking mouth any second. Still, in all, she was cool.

She pulled off her glasses and said grace before we started eating. Quanessa held my hand and her daughter's tightly. Ms. Baron smiled.

"You know how long I've been waiting for this girl to get married?" Ms. Baron began.

"Mommy, please," Quanessa interrupted.

"Oh hush. Be happy you got yourself a rich, good-looking man. A black man that paid for his own wedding. Shit . . . you sure you married the right Ms. Baron?" she smiled.

"I'm sure." Though in my mind, I was more like, damn skippy! Freaking troll.

"Well if you ever change your mind—"

"I'm quite sure this is forever, Ms. Baron."

"You tell her, boo," Quanessa said kissing me.

"Do y'all gotta be doing all that at the table?" Tyeesha complained.

"They in love, girl. Now you just hush your mouth and eat that cauliflower," her grandmother snapped.

After dinner, we went to the family room. Tyeesha bounced to the bedroom to talk on the jack. I was too tired to go back home tonight, so we stayed.

"I have good news, boo," Quanessa said, as we lay in bed.

"What's that?"

"I'm being promoted to head nurse, but the position is in New York. It pays so much more."

"Well it really doesn't matter how much they pay, because I got all the money you need for you and Tyeesha."

"That's really sweet, Mark. It really is, but I do like having my own."

"Why is it that when a nigga has no doe, there's always a fucking complaint? Then when he got doe, there's still a complaint?"

"Boo, lower your voice, okay? Secondly, don't cuss at me. I don't cuss at you. This is a discussion we're having."

"So what you trying to say, Quanessa? You want to move to New York?"

"I'm not sure. This is all so sudden. I didn't even know I was up for promotion. It wouldn't be until next year anyway. Like sometime in February."

Man, she just didn't know; I could never go back to New York. Damn, Santiago! But the D's would nab me fo'sho. Maybe even murk a nigga. I know mad cats were after me too. Naw. Naw. No! No New York.

"Mark, are you listening to me?"

"Yeah," I said, although I had stopped listening five minutes ago.

"So?"

"I'd have to think about it, Nessa."

"Don't play with me, boy. What's going on? You got a girl or baby's mother up there?"

"I wish it were that simple. It's a long story." She folded her arms and sat up against the wall.

"Well you're in luck because we just so happen to have the rest of our lives."

"Baby, I can't say just yet, but it's nothing to do with bitches and babies."

"Are you sure?"

"Yes."

"You know I trust you right?"

"Yes."

"You promise to never let me and mines get hurt?"

"Momma, I swear before God and one of three wise

men. I'll never let anything happen to you and your shorty.
Our shorty. We're married now, she's my daughter too."
My cell rang. It was Dre at the club with the connect.
Quanessa was not going to be happy with this, but money
comes first. If she couldn't understand that, then oh fuck-
ing well.

"Baby. It's the club. They need me down there."

"I thought you were on vacation."

"This is big business, baby. There is no such thing as
vacation. I'll meet you back at the condo tomorrow,
okay?"

"No. It's not okay. But if you have to be there, then you
have to be there."

"I'm sorry, ma."


I was supposed to meet with Dre at the coffee shop on
the corner from the all-night carwash. There he was inside talking to a man, sporting a powder-blue fisherman
hat, a green, short-sleeved Polo shirt, and tan shorts. He
kind of smelled like a cop. I walked inside the shop and
over to the table where Dre and the man sat.

"What's good, Dre?" I asked giving him dap.

"Ain't nothing. This my nigga that be bringing in the
profit dawg," he said to the connect. The man stared in
my eyes for a moment.

"Something the matter, partna?" I asked him.

"My name is Kilaneega. You and your brother have
been making me a very rich man."

"Not me and my brother man. Me! I make the shit go
'round."

"Whatever. Can you move fifteen kilos in a week?"

"Fo'sho."

"Good. Say. You look familiar. Ever been to New
York?"

"Naw, homie. I was born and raised round these here parts. So how we gonna do this?"

"Same pattern as always. Except now you deal with me and me only. Dre is going back home for awhile. Things are getting real hot these days. You just can't tell who's a cop anymore," he laughed.

# CHAPTER THIRTY-THREE

## *Carmello*

"What's up, Caine? Why you got me up so late at night? Shouldn't you be home with your wife?" I asked my brother, as we sat in my living room. The expression on his face was a happy one, but I just couldn't shake the feeling that he was about to announce some ol' bullshit to me.

"What if I told you that around this time next year, you could be a millionaire again?"

"No! No! No!" I stood up shaking my head back and forth. "Haven't you learned anything from the past?"

"Yeah! I learned to be more careful."

"Apparently you haven't. You have a wife and a child now. I can't believe you'd risk it all. You do remember that we're fugitives, right?" This nigga!

"You know what, Mello? I tripped before when you wouldn't at least give my idea a chance. But when you did, I felt like we were Batman and Robin again. You know, side by side, whooping asses and shit."

"You been pushing inside the club?" I interrogated.

He looked to the floor then back up again.

"Yeah. How you think we were able to afford all the renovations and celebrities? That shit costs. But you see how much we make back? We ain't never had it like this, dun."

"Damn it, Caine. Why can't you get this through your thick skull? I don't want to do this anymore!" I yelled, banging my fists on my head.

"Why, nigga? You don't like dirty money anymore? You should. You was raised on it."

"Yo, fuck the past, Caine. I'm tired of hearing about that shit. I wouldn't even be in this predicament if it weren't for you."

"Aww naw nigga—nigga, don't pin the tail on me. You the big brother. Accept your responsibilities. I'm just following your example."

"What example is that?"

"How to look out for number one dawg."

"Why you always talking shit, huh?"

"Fuck you, punk," he said closing in. We stared down for about two minutes in complete silence, with the exception of the blue plastic-bladed G.E. fan. He smiled and patted my chest.

"Damn, boy. Those nose hairs be flaring when you tight. So, nigga, it seems we have a small dilemma. You don't want drugs in the building, and I already got them there. What ya going to do? Call the cops?" He fiendishly laughed.

I stared at his dumb ass. He was going to fuck everything up. I wasn't trying to do two minutes locked up. This nigga was not going to have my ass shipped up north for drugs and murder. I could have sworn a car was following me around all day too. Every car that slowed down in front of me was suspect in my eyes. I'll take down two before they hit this one, for real, because I don't do jail or caskets. I'm claustrophobic. Know what I mean? As much as I loved this man something had to be done.

"Caine, I'll sign you over full power of the club right now."

"No the fuck you won't, nigga. We in this together, until our walls come crashing down."

"Baby boy, it's over now. It's just me and you. You can cut out the thug life routine."

"Routine? Routine? Nigga, I was born a thug. Straight gangsta. Look at me. I been through war. Shot. Stabbed. Hunted by police. I'm out here smacking bitches' men in the face for them. I do's the damn thang thoroughly my man."

"You sound stupid as hell, Caine. Really though, get out the movie, nigga."

"Oh, you think it's the movies? I'ma show you the movies. I'm out. I'll be here to sign the papers for the club tomorrow."

He walked out slamming the door behind him. *Damn it, Caine. Why the fuck is you tripping out?* Motherfucka. I gotta keep an eye on that nigga again.

Ring. Ring.

"Hello? What? How do you know my name?" I asked the unfamiliar voice on the other end of the phone. "Hello? Hello?"

# CHAPTER THIRTY-FOUR

## *Santiago*

"Are you sure that's where he lives, Senorita Francis?" Santiago asked Federal Agent Jasmine Gurthy a.k.a. Cynthia Francis. He was sitting in the front seat of his good friend Raul's Porsche, using binoculars to focus in on Carmello's new life. "Does he have money in the house?"

"No," the undercover agent answered.

"Droga?"

"No."

"Very good, agent. Your money will be in its usual place."

Santiago knew of Gurthy when Carlos first got pinched. He made her an offer. Now she worked on both sides of the law. She figured if she was going to risk her life everyday, she may as well get paid real money to risk it. She'd been on the Santiago investigation for six years. She'd never actually witnessed any transactions with him involved personally, but she had witnessed over fifty homicides committed by him. She was commanded by her superiors to only report large amounts of paraphernalia. When she did finally get her opportunity to witness the transactions, she would flip the script on Santiago, then retrieve the over $8 million that she had gradually accrued by skimming from his enormous monthly intake.

Of course this was accrued by saving over the past six years. She kept it hidden in a hole under the deck of her brother's home in Virginia. She had it all figured out. When the bust went down, she'd make her move, but there was a new job that Santiago had for her today.

"I've been wondering, agent, have you fucked Carmello yet?"

"No. And I'm not going to."

"You do it as a special favor for me, okay? I'll give you a bonus. And I'll even throw in some information about the brother team that is responsible for that killing spree in New York and Virginia two years ago."

"If you know where he's at, you should tell me anyway. I can make things real hot for you too, sir."

"Ha. Ha. Such joy and laughter, agent. Aren't you standing in your bedroom window just pulling your bra over those big black tits?" There was silence.

"What is it I have to do?" she asked closing her blinds, and cautiously moving away from the window.

"All you have to do is fuck him. I want his last memories to be happy. His brother won't be as fortunate when I see him."

Santiago hung up the phone and enjoyed the peaceful ride to Raul's small home. It was the perfect hideaway. He could kill Carmello, Caine, Agent Gurthy, and the one man who could still bring him down if he ever rose from his hideaway. Uncle Todd.

Todd swindled Santiago out of a lot of money right before Carmello Sr. and Juanita were to leave for Cancun. He was gone before Santiago could catch him, so he assumed they were all in it together. Respect goes a long way, but thievery cuts the lifespan short. He felt bad after discovering that they weren't the culprits, but business is business. Life goes on. All Santiago knew was if he failed the simple mission his father gave him, he surely would be exiled from the cartel. His very own children would surely die by the hands of their very own grandfather. Santiago would kill him first before he ever laid a hand on his family. After murdering his own father, he could resume all power. He had it all figured out. He had to meet up with another dirty cop in a half an hour named Kilaneega. What joy Santiago felt, when Kilaneega informed him that he'd be meeting with Caine Saturday night at the club. Just as he'd promised Agent Gurthy, there was a reward for Kilaneega's assistance.

"You see how they are in America, Raul? Dirty. Greedy. No honor. Money is the only thing they care about. In America you can buy anything, even the presidency." Santiago continued to school Raul before savoring the forkful of spicy jerk pork.

# CHAPTER THIRTY-FIVE

## *Caine*

Despite our differences, Mello found a house for me and my new family to live in. I also purchased a small boat to fish in for the next summer. We put the honeymoon off until next summer when Quanessa could get a longer vacation. From time to time, she brought up the New York move. There was going to be no getting around telling her the true story. I didn't want to lose her, which would more than likely be the end result, once I confessed my past demons to her. But it was going to be now or never. I waited until Tyeesha left with her friends.

"Quanessa?" I called. She walked out of the kitchen, sipping a glass of juice.

"What's up?"

"Sit down, I have something I need to talk to you about." A concerned look grew on her face.

"I'm listening."

"There's no easy way to say this, ma, but we can't go to New York. We just can't."

"Mark, it's what I want to do. I have goals."

"I understand all of that, sweetness, but if we make that move, it may be the last time we see each other."

"What kind of crazy you talking?"

"I don't even know where to begin."

"How about from the beginning?" Pausing for a moment, I inhaled deeply and squeezed her hand tightly.

"Promise you won't hate me?"

"You're scaring me, Mark. What is it?"

In the nick of time, the phone rang. It was her doctor. It gave me more than enough time to dismantle the confidence I'd built up to snitch on myself. It would just be too much for her to know that she married a murdering, drug-dealing, child-killer. She didn't even know my official name. Fuck! She didn't even have my middle name.

"Mark?" she smiled. "Baby, we're pregnant."

"Pregnant? Me?"

"Us baby. Four months."

"Say word," I said spinning her around ecstatically.

"Now what were you about to say earlier about New York?"

"Nothing, babe. Nothing at all."

"So you're saying we can move there?"

"Next year. Let's just save a little more money."

"I love you, Mark Jackson."

"I love you too."

"Tyeesha will be so surprised. Why don't you take her out tonight, babe. She really likes you."

"I like her too. I guess she's like the teenaged daughter I never had."

She actually reminded me of China.

"You so silly."

Tyeesha was a wild little girl. I guess Quanessa thought some of what I had to offer would rub off on her, being that we were connected to the same generation.

Isn't that ironic? I let her drive my brand new, purple painted Lexus drop-top that went from zero to one hundred and sixty in five seconds. We pumped the shit out of the newly installed Bose system, and played connect the dots with the equalizer until the bass satisfied our taste. We sped through the Miami streets with no fear of five-o until we reached the weed spot. We stepped out the car looking like super-stars. She was popular now because I was popular. I bought her a whole new wardrobe and was planning on buying her a whip of her very own for her birthday next week. After copping the trees, we went to the boardwalk and sat on the benches. After rolling the dutch, we began puffing.

"I'm glad you married my moms, man. You cool," she complemented.

"You cool too, Shawdy. I like the way our relationship is. If you ever got anything you wanna talk about and you can't talk to Nessa about it, I'm your nigga."

"True that?"

"I'm serious. Anybody give you flack, you come to me and I'll handle the shit, okay?"

"Yeah," she answered, passing the L. She started bopping her head in sync with the ol' school song by Tupac.

"Tyeesha, your moms just told me today that she's pregnant."

"For real yo? Seriously?"

"No question, ma. You about to be a big sister."

"Oh shit. Hell yeah!" she screamed puffing the L again.

"I guess that means you're alright with it?"

"Show ya right."

"The reason why I brought you out tonight, ma, is because me and your moms thought it would be good for us to spend some quality time together."

"Yeah, but it ain't no thang. We good."

"Even so, you need to chill on these streets. You be hittin' them real hard."

"I'm straight."

"You straight?"

"As a rehabilitated criminal," she laughed. My phone rang. Always the interruptions.

It was Alex from the club. He said there was a dude asking for me by my official name. I told him to handle it and I'd see him tomorrow night, but he said the dude wouldn't leave until I got there. Our house was completely in the opposite direction from where we were, so I had to take Tyeesha with me.

I parked in front of the club and told her to take the car home through the back streets. There was a small crowd encircling Alex and some little nigga he had hemmed up. He struggled to free himself, but Alex had him tight. The flashing party lights momentarily concealed his identity until he was dragged into the light. It was little Larry from New York. I don't know how he found me, but he wasn't going back home tonight, tomorrow, or ever.

"Bring his ass upstairs," I said.

He had a small crew of four with him. None of the niggas I'd ever seen before. My peoples inside chased them out of the club and down the block. Four of us, including Alex, were fucking little Larry up in the elevator.

"What the fuck are you doing here nigga? How'd you find me?" He laughed while blood flooded his mouth, and wounds opened all over his face.

"Who this nigga?" Alex asked.

"This faggot-ass punk from back home popped me in the leg two years ago."

"Word? What you doing here, little nigga?" Alex yelled, dragging him out of the elevator by the neck. Little Larry struggled to no avail. Alex's death-grip was clenched too tight around his pencil-sized neck. After getting him in the office, he was thrown to the floor.

"Y'all, get back down to the door. Make sure no one else gets past," I said to the smaller guards. I closed the door behind them and locked it.

"You got real balls, nigga. Put that nigga in the chair," I said. Alex forced him to the chair and pointed his .45 at him.

"It's all over, Caine. We know everything. You killed Chantell, Starks, Sunshine, and my brother, muthafucka. Did you have to take out his family too?"

"Fuck you talking about your brother?"

"Monty, Nigga! That brother!" he yelled, spitting up blood. "You had to go and murder his girl and kids too, right?"

"What? You five-o now? You wearing a wire or something?" I yelled pulling at his button-up shirt. I exposed his bare chest, it was clear.

"Strip!" I said. As he got down to his boxers, he stopped.

"Keep going, nigga. Did I tell you to stop?" He stripped naked and was clean. So now the question was, what was he doing here in Miami? In my club? How'd he find me? More importantly, how'd he know about the murders?

"I want you to look at your work boy," I said unbuckling my belt. I pulled down my pants. "See how fucked up my shit look? You shouldn't have come here."

"Nigga, it don't matter if you kill me or not. Your number is coming up."

"Your number is coming up too, but before you die, nigga, tell me why you here and how you found me?"

"I ain't telling you shit. Just know this? Me and Monty weren't the only ones you had to wet, bitch," he said, spitting a mouthful of blood on me.

"Yo, gimme that shit" I said to Alex, reaching for the gun. "Now look at you. Sitting here at gunpoint, faggot!"

"I'm sorry, Monty. I tried to be there for you," he said looking towards the ceiling.

"You looking in the wrong direction," I said pointing towards the floor. "Tell that faggot-ass brother of yours I said hi. Kiss the wife and kids for me too," I added before piercing his chest four times with the peace-maker. "Stupid muthafucka. I'm Caine, nigga. You don't gotta ask nobody. Just try me. Call the boys up, so they can slide this bitch outta here," I said.

Alex made the call and they arrived minutes later.

"Burn his body and dump it. Anybody know the niggas he was with?" I asked.

"Yeah. They be in the pool-hall every Friday night," Simba answered.

"I'm saying though, do you know them?" I asked him again.

"Naw. Not like that."

"Good. Take care of it. They gonna be looking for his ass soon."

"We just gonna drive by and spray thangs," Simba said.

"Whatever. Handle your business. Call me when it's done."

Shit. I was tired of getting my hands dirty. Why should I have to when I got niggas I could pay to do it for me? Nothing was gonna stop me from getting that paper.

# CHAPTER THIRTY-SIX

## *Carmello*

"This nigga never home," complained Cynthia about her boyfriend.

"Nigga be handling thangs," I said.

"He be handling shit. I think he be fucking around."

"On you? He'd be a fool to cheat on your ass. For real."

"Think so?"

"I know so."

"You better stop before you put yourself in a good predicament." She smiled.

"I don't fuck around in another man's home. That shit is foul."

"Fuck him. He don't appreciate me. I just handle his day to day."

"So leave him."

"And go where?"

"You got doe. Just bounce out the state."

"That's some pretty harsh advice coming from a concerned Samaritan who doesn't fuck around in another man's home."

"You're the one complaining. I'm just trying to help."

"You want to help me, Mr. Jackson?"

"If I can."

"Make love to me."

"Can't do that, babe."

"Why not? You a faggot or something?"

"Naw. I just don't like tarnished goods."

"You'd pass this up because of your ethics?"

"Getting pussy is for teenagers. I don't just rest my head next to a bitch anymore. Unless I feel for her."

"You don't feel me?"

"That's not what I said. You're not mine. So I don't touch."

"That's some faggot shit. You just afraid this love is going to infect you with that jones."

"You bugging. I'ma be out." I turned to walk away, but she grabbed my arm.

"Wait. I love you," she said.

"Cynthia, you wilding out. Your man could be home any minute."

"Stop being so righteous and have some fun for once in your life, boy."

We walked to her room and sat at the foot of the bed. She massaged the back of my neck, while I forcefully fought the urge to twist her back out.

"I'm so hot for you, boo," she said, licking my chin full-tongued.

"You're making this real hard, Cynthia."

"I hope that's not all I'm making hard." She rubbed my crotch up and down. Finally surrendering, I leaned back on the king-sized mattress, while she licked the inside of my navel. She began unbuttoning my shirt from the bottom.

"Let me pull the curtains and close the window. People might hear us."

"So what. You scared?" she asked.

"If you don't care, I don't either."

"Good. I want them to hear us. It'll mean you handling your business."

For the first time, I saw Cynthia's bare body. Every curve and muscle was toned to perfection. Her thick calves flexed as she squatted over my love. The tight, wet, and warm dwelling I'd entered stimulated my staff of thickness. She appreciated the length and width, which sent shock waves through her hips. With each whirl and gyration of her secret garden, her juices increased and boiled, causing me to slip out every once in awhile and accidentally poke in her brown sugar. She loved it. Placing me back inside of her, she laid on her back. I knew I was positioned correctly the instant she jumped. I'd made friction with her very visible clitoris, which wet her vaginal lawn from being so hot. She vigorously began rubbing her two fingers down below, as I began to trace the dark outer rings of her nipples with my tongue. She then began rubbing my piece back across her love to keep her wet. I followed with my head to where her hand was and sniffed the sweet drops of cherry dew sitting between her thighs and on her fingers. I placed both her hands at her side as she trembled in anticipation.

With my tongue stretched out as far as it could go, I placed her clit on the back of my tongue near the tonsils and licked forward sensuously, seductively, and slowly. Her legs catapulted in the air and bent at the knees with her red toenails curling up. She bit her bottom lip and dug her naturally long fingernails into my shoulders. We proceeded pleasuring one another's sensitive spots of passion with mouths, hands, words, and irresistible physical tools of indulgence. This continued from sundown to moonrise. After being drained of our energies, we laid out in the nude on top of blue exercise mats on the second floor deck. It overlooked the beach in the distance.

"That was crazy," I smiled.

"Yeah. That was real. If I didn't know any better, I'd think you were putting feeling behind your effort," she probed.

"My only concern was to make sure you got yours. That's why niggas lose their woman. They always trying to get theirs first."

"So you was sent here to do the job right, huh?"

"I didn't say all that. I just want a woman to know how much I appreciate her warmth. Her scent. Her taste."

"You about to start some shit up again. I don't think you want that."

"What now, Cynthia?"

"What now, what?" she asked.

"It's obvious we have feelings for each other. How are we going to work this? I mean with you having a man and all?"

"You let me take care of that. I'll come up with something. How is Mark coming along with the club since you signed it over to him?"

"I ain't spoke to him since. I guess he's doing alright."

"What is the issue with you two? Two brothers in business down to one."

"Maybe one day I can explain it to you in full detail. It's just that now's not the right time."

"Why do men always say that shit?"

"Probably because it don't be the right time."

"Whatever. You don't trust me or something? You think I'm after your money? I got my own. Why won't you open up to me? You know so much about me already."

"You chose to volunteer that information. I didn't ask you shit."

Cynthia's house phone rang. She wrapped the blanket we were sharing around her bottom and answered the call inside the den. She closed the sliding patio door behind her. She winked at me as she talked on the phone. Hanging it up and sliding the door open half-way, she used the free hand to continue securing the blanket around her.

"Boo?" she began, "I have some business to take care of. Like in the next twenty minutes. You're going to have to shower at home."

I stood up with my dick in my hand massaging its head with my thumb, maintaining its erectility. As I walked in towards her, she turned her back and walked to the bathroom, quickly closing the door behind her.

"That's cold," I said.

# CHAPTER THIRTY-SEVEN

## *The Set Up Crew*

Agent Gurthy, Detective Kilaneega, and Agent Berry, a.k.a Dre, all sat in a back office of the library in a secret location drinking coffee. Each was satisfied with the amount of time and progress they put into the operation of bringing down Santiago's drug ring, and the Denn brothers reign of fame. Especially Caine's. They were teaming up tonight with Miami's finest to raid Caine's club. A hot tip given by a reliable informant gave them further insight into the recent wave of coke deaths these past four weeks. Two out of every six packages were being cut with rat poison.

There were also rumors of a surveillance tape floating around showing Gurthy's youngest brother, Larry, being dragged into an elevator by Caine's head of security and never returning. Weeks earlier, Agent Cynthia Gurthy and Larry Gurthy, who was a New York City officer, had devised a plan to kill Caine during a bust while purchasing from Dre through Kilaneega, who had been distributed to by Santiago. All three agents were on Santiago's payroll and led him to Caine and Carmello's whereabouts. Caine definitely was going to pay for murdering her oldest brother Monty and his family. She was going to do it her way, then clean him and Carmello out.

For the rest of the plan to go off without a hitch, one more operative would be needed—a person who knew Carmello and Caine better than they might've known themselves. The only other person who could supply the Supreme Court with enough information to bring the Decosta Cartel to its knees was Uncle Todd. Uncle Todd had disappeared into the witness protection program back in 1995, after skating off with almost $2 million dollars of Santiago's money. He was upset with Carmello Sr. and his sister-in-law for dissolving such a lucrative partnership so early in their career. He was expected to take Santiago the last of his money, but decided out of spite for his brother's selfish actions, to rob Santiago and let the blame rest where it may. Not only had he disappeared with Santiago's money, but he also emptied the monies from his brother's safe in Westchester. At that point Santiago was so angered that niggers would even dare to rob him after all the opportunities he'd provided them, that he decided they could only reimburse him with their lives.

When they arrived at the airport, Carlos and his goons were waiting in the front with two limousines. Each driver got out of the ebony chariots and opened the golden handles of the doors. It was complicated to detect that this was an abduction in progress at the time. Neither Carmello nor Juanita was aware that Todd had jerked them and Santiago. They were only advised to hurry into the limo.

"What's this all about, Carlos? We have a flight to catch in about twenty minutes," Carmello Sr. said looking down at his watch.

"Baby. You forgot the sun-tan lotion," Juanita said, reexamining the contents of the suitcase for the sixth time since they'd left home.

"Don't worry about the lotion right now sweetheart. We have bigger problems," Carlos said.

"Like what? Tell Santiago my decision is final. I'm out for good," said Carmello Sr.

"You're going to stand there and act like you don't know what this is all about?" Carlos asked Carmello Sr.

"You sniffing the product again, Carlos?" Juanita asked.

"Santiago is very disappointed in the two of you. I told him to never trust a mono. Where is that brother of yours, Carmello? Did you actually believe Santiago would not miss over $2 million dollars? You fucking thieves." Carmello and Juanita looked at one another already knowing where the missing money went. It was gone. Right along with Todd. Carmello could've just simply reimbursed Santiago, but Santiago didn't want the money back. He wanted revenge. No one was going to play him.

Carlos had the chauffeur drive to a deserted area. It appeared to be an old junkyard not far from the airport. Jumbo jets flew over their heads every other ten minutes. No sounds could be heard coming from the area. Not even gunshots. Juanita cried as she thought of her children. She felt bad about putting China on punishment last week for smoking weed in the church's bathroom. She would never see Mello graduate from college. She'd have to depend on Mello's parental suaveness to keep Caine from doing a life bid in prison.

"Damn, Todd!" she said out loud. A white limousine pulled up thirty minutes later. Santiago emerged from the white stallion aiming his gun.

"You dirty muthafuckas steal from me? Me?" he shouted.

"You got it all wrong, Santiago," Carmello Sr. said.

"Really? Then tell me what is right?" But Carmello would never rat on anyone, especially not his own brother. He rationalized in his heart that this was the price to be paid when you invested in dirt. The loving couple of twenty years stood side by side, holding hands. Juanita was too bold for tears, but shed them anyway. Not because she was going to die, but because of the area and the circumstances she was to be executed under. Carmello wrapped his arm around her shoulder and pulled her close.

"I want to know where my money is, Carmello. Where is your brother? Did he take it?"

"I don't know what you're talking about."

"Oh, you do not? Tell me where your brother is and maybe I let you live."

"I can't do that because I don't know where he is. Even if I did, I wouldn't tell you."

"That is too bad, Senior Carmello. I was nice enough to let you and your family pack up and leave me, only because you were such a modest man. I was willing to risk losing that extra million a week. But this is how you do business? You fuck me in the culata? But no! I'm going to fuck you. Your nenes will work for me until the day they die. Both of you remove all of your clothing. Ahora!" They both stood motionless.

"Ahora!" Santiago yelled, shooting at their feet. For fear of Juanita's life, Carmello Sr. began to hastily undo his pants. Juanita followed. As Juanita pulled off her T-shirt, her huge breasts bounced up and down. Carlos smiled at them, while approaching Juanita. With a devilish grin, he kissed them both.

"Grande tits, mami," Carlos said, admiring their perfect shape and size.

"If you touch her, I will kill you," Carmello defended.

Carlos took a couple of steps backwards and looked down at Carmello Sr.'s dick.

"How do you fit that big shit in her chor-cha?" he asked. "My cock isn't that big. I'm jealous. Why should you have mucho balls and I have peanuts? I know how to fix that." Carlos shot Carmello Sr. in the nuts without a moment's hesitation. Juanita screamed and cried, but it went unheard due to the overhead jet engines taking off.

Carmello crumpled to the ground in a fetal position. His naked body now covered in brownish-yellow dirt from rolling back and forth in excruciating pain. Blood poured from his mouth causing him to spittle and choke. No longer able to endure her annoying cries of fear and terror, Santiago walked up to Juanita and let off a slug into her forehead. She fell with her arms spread wide next to her dying husband. Santiago kicked dirt into Carmello Sr.'s face.

"Turn over, punta," he said. Carmello turned on his back, still holding his nuts, and grimacing in the worst pain any man would ever experience in his whole entire life. Stepping down on his chest, Santiago aimed appropriately.

"The only thing worse than a nigger, is a nigger who steals from me," Santiago said before extinguishing Carmello's last spark of life.

After the murder of his brother and sister-in-law, Todd became fearful for his very own life. Although he'd be capable of evading Santiago's men for awhile, he was very aware of the fact that he wouldn't be able to hide forever, so he took everything he knew about the Decosta cartel to the FBI. They, in turn, promised him safe housing, providing his information would lead to the downfall of the notorious mob. But Santiago's paper was just too long. Every agent that was sent to bring him down was paid a wealthy chunk of change to continue turning their heads. Now after eight years he'd finally have his revenge. Todd was a dead man. He'd cost him so much time, money, and embarrassment. Just one trip to Miami and it would all be over. Then his father would once again look at him like a real man. He wouldn't be some dumb immigrant, picking beans just so some lazy, caffeine-addicted American could drink the liquids of his labor, while poking fun at the obvious poverty-stricken picture of Pablo and his overweight mule on the red coffee can.

# CHAPTER THIRTY-EIGHT

## *Caine*

After Simba and his men dumped Larry's body and sprayed the pool hall, five-o never gave the block a moment's rest. It turned out that Larry was a cop back in New York. They had no witnesses or leads to the perpetrator, but it did make the spot hot just when things were really beginning to pick up. Everybody was coming to the club just to cop coke. There was so much money being made, that I eventually had to convince Tyeesha to hide some of the money in her bank account. Only I had access to the account, but she could have however much she wanted within reason. That lead to a lot of questions from her. She soon forgot all about it when I bought her a 2007 burgundy Escalade for her birthday. I sent her mother on that vacation in Italy she always wanted and bought us a very expensive home in an upscale part of Miami.

Money made everybody happy. Quanessa was really beginning to show now. Shit really couldn't have looked better. Even me and Mello were on speaking terms again.

He didn't know it, but I had a secret account for him too where money was just piling up.

"Yeah, man. I had to do that nigga. I didn't know he was the beast though," I explained to Dre, as we sat in the family room of my home sipping E&J.

"Damn, nigga. That's real."

"Then Simba had to go spray the block because the niggas he was with that night hung out there. Smoked all them cats too, boy."

"Word? That's real talk homie."

"Yeah. Niggas try'na knock me out the box. But I ain't having it. Feel me, dawg?"

"I feel ya, man. So Alex coming with us tonight to get that?"

"No question. That's my strong-arm nigga. He got my back."

"You the man, nigga. Everybody got your back."

"That's right," I said, cleaning my .357.

We went to do the pick-up at the club. We had to shut down for a week until things cooled off. Alex opened the doors and we all entered. Kilaneega suspiciously observed the darkened surroundings before the lights were turned on. We walked to the far end of the club, towards the mirrored walls. There we sat at the six-man VIP table. Alex immediately thereafter sought to retrieve the three briefcases of funds. Kilaneega sat close to Dre studying us hard after he returned. He placed one on the table and two at his feet. He took a step backwards with his hand on his holster.

"Where he at?" I asked.

"He's always on time. You nervous?" Kilaneega challenged.

"Never that."

"Relax then. It'll all be over soon." That's when he received the ring on his phone. He spoke briefly then hung up. He stared at the doors and nodded his head. Alex looked at me for confirmation. Cautiously he headed toward the unsecured door and kicked it open. Before the shadowed silhouette could move, he was snatched off his feet. Alex quickly looked around the outside perimeter, before closing the door and locking it.

"Easy, easy," Kilaneega said.

"This your boy?" I asked.

"No. Actually it's your uncle." As I inspected his shaven face and head, it began retracting memories of way back when. Tears began falling from my eyes, and transformed to anger in my heart.

"It's been a long time, Caine," he said, extending his hand as if we were cool.

"Not long enough muthafucka. This where you been hiding at all this time? Just chilling in Miami. What the fuck is he doing here, Kilaneega?" I yelled reaching for my gun. Dre and Kilaneega simultaneously pulled out on me.

"What the fuck, y'all? What's this about?" The door opened again. Before Alex could hold it down, he was shot in the leg while my ex-partners in crime kept me at bay. The figure swayed in with a familiar swagger in the hips. It was Mello's girl, Cynthia. This time she locked the doors and hit the lights, with the exception of the few overhead.

"What? Y'all gonna rob me now? I put y'all on the map. And why this nigga here blowing up my name?" I looked at Todd. He turned his head. Fuck it. I been in this situation before. Or maybe not.

"Yo, Dre, man. What's good baby? You gonna let this go down?"

"You know what, Caine? Caine Denn, right?"

"What the fuck is going on?" I yelled again.

"You talk too much, Caine. That's what the fuck is

going on," Kilaneega answered. "You talk way, way too much. You think just because you changed your name and cut your hair we wouldn't find you? Child-killer."

He slapped me in the face with the butt of his gun.

"You can't do this to me."

"We can do anything we want. We're the FBI, homeboy."

Alex lay motionless on the cold dark-green marble floor, while Agent Gurthy dug her knee deep inside his back with her gun kissing the rear of his head.

"Just give me a reason," she threatened him.

"So y'all all FEDS?" I asked.

"Seven days a week, all year long, hustler," Dre said, suddenly losing that rough Texan accent.

"I wanna see proof," I insisted.

"Like I said, Caine, you talk too much," Kilaneega said, producing a recorder with me confessing to Little Larry about the murders in New York and Virginia. Dre was also wearing a wire that night, but the ultimate proof was the recording of me popping Larry in the chest four times. They, including Todd, sat around the edges of the table grilling me. But what the fuck did Todd have to do with all of this?

"That shit don't mean nothing. I got lawyers to shake that shit. Anyway, what the fuck do you have to do with all this Todd?"

"Well, ol' boy, it's like this. They're all working for Santiago. He helps them bust the big shipments." I jumped out my chair.

"Santiago? Here?" I asked surprised.

"What's the matter, Thug-life? You shook? Santiago gives them the dirt on competing connections and the government, in turn, lets Santiago run his business with no interference; providing that he can also pay the government drug trade taxes. I been here in Miami ever since Mello and your momma was buried. After I stole Santiago's money from your mommy and daddy, I just ran and never looked back. Good thing the Feds caught me before Santiago.

After a year in prison for drug-abuse and distribution, I was released. Gave up everything they needed to know about what I knew on your father. But as luck would have it, I ran into Santiago soon after. He said all would be forgiven if I led him to your parents and began working for him immediately."

"But why, dawg? Why? He was your brother. My father."

"Your father made all his money and didn't care about who else had what. We were partners and he just up and left me broke."

"Bullshit!"

"Fuck all of this bull. You killed both my brothers, asshole!" screamed Agent Gurthy. "And you don't think you're going down?" she asked, lifting her gun to my head.

Alex lay frozen-stiff on the floor, with his hands stretched out in front of him.

"Come on, Gurthy, we're not done yet," Dre intervened.

"Yeah. We still gotta pick up this scum bucket's brother, the infamous Mr. Jackson, better known as Carmello Jr. Hey? While we're here we might as well go ahead and get a head start on finding all this coke I've been hearing about," suggested Kilaneega.

"Are you guys fucking deaf? My brothers were murdered by this scum. I want to do him myself," Gurthy said.

"Does my brother know you a cop? Do you suck his dick with the safety on or off?" I asked Cynthia with a frown. Dre punched me in the mouth.

"You better watch it, thug, or I'll let the lady have her way with you."

"Fuck you! Uncle Tom-ass nigga." I spit on his shoes. He pulled my black bandana from around my head, and wiped the green glob of goo off the tip of his Sean John sneakers.

"You can't even sell drugs correctly, punk. You kill kids. You shoot pregnant women and you're a cop-killer. You're looking at a real long time, dick," Dre said. All the while Cynthia continued stepping down on the back of Alex's neck.

"This is how it's going to work, Caine," Gurthy began, "Santiago will be here soon under the impression that we're going to let him kill you. He also will have twenty bricks for Todd over here. After we see the drugs and he makes the threat against your life, we'll move in and apprehend him."

"What? Y'all think I'm stupid or something? Why not just arrest him for the drugs alone?" I asked.

"It is taking every bit of morality inside myself to stop from killing you myself. So your best bet is to follow the plan, or you can die here and now."

"The decision is yours," Kilaneega added. As I weighed my options, it was obvious that they were ultimately limited.

"What exactly is it that I have to do?"

"Start by telling me why you killed my brothers?" Gurthy demanded.

"You know the game. It's all about territory."

"What part does Carmello play in this all?"

"Mello plays no part. Why does everybody think he's the mastermind behind everything? This is mine."

"It really doesn't matter. You won't be running shit from under the jail. You hear that, Alex? Jail! You willing to do twenty-five years for this shit-head?"

"The only thing I did was hold the man down in the chair," he said.

"Shut up, Lex. I got this. They don't got shit on us."

"Fuck that! I ain't doing nobody's bid. What else y'all need to know?" Alex said.

He began to confess every transaction and murder that he could tie to me, just to save his own neck. His "No Snitch" T-shirt was revoked. He was then allowed to stand up freely. He gave me an apologetic look and I turned my head on him. He already knew that if we ever made it out of this alive, I'd see him again and snuff his miserable life out. Nobody liked a snitch. Shit. Even cops didn't respect cops that told on other cops.

"What now?" Alex asked no one in particular.

"Now?" Kilaneega asked. "You get to go home."

"Just like that?"

"You didn't pull the trigger, right?"

"Naw. That nigga did it," he answered, pointing at me without looking.

"Then get your ass out of here. I don't ever want to see you in Miami again. Everything you've heard here tonight, stays in here. Got it?" Dre and Gurthy looked at one another puzzled, as Alex headed towards the exit without hesitation.

"Hey, Alex?" called Kilaneega. "You really think it's that easy? You just told on your own boy to save your ass. What will you do to us?"

"Aww, come on, man. I won't say shit. Caine? Say something!" he begged me.

"Fuck you, man. Shit on me? Kill'em," I said, turning my head and heart.

"Y'all can't do this," he cried.

"Why can't we?" Kilaneega asked.

"Because it ain't right."

"Man, we the police. Ain't nothing we do right," Dre

laughed. Kilaneega followed in with more laughter. Alex tried to force the door open, but was blasted twice in the back by Kilaneega.

"Catch," he said, quickly tossing the gun to me. "That gun is from ballistics with the serial number scratched off. It has your fingerprints all over it now, pal. You've been on one hell of a killing spree over the past two years. You're going to help us bring that asshole Santiago down. Or, we can just let him kill you and your new family. How's that sound, Caine?"

"It sounds like some real grimy shit."

"You ain't heard nothing yet. After we bust Santiago, you and your brother are going to empty out those dummy accounts and give the money to us. Are we clear?"

"You'll have forty-eight hours before you and Carmello's identities are released to the public. After that, you are on your own," Gurthy said.

"I'm sorry, nephew," Todd said. "Should I make the call?" he asked Kilaneega.

# CHAPTER THIRTY-NINE

## *Carmello*

I had this funny feeling about Cynthia. Something just didn't seem to make sense. For instance, her sudden appearance out of nowhere and her moves in and out of the state several times a week. The way she constantly nagged me about divulging in-depth history of my past. I thought about this long and hard as I lay in her bed, awaiting her arrival from Seattle. As the morning sun shined through the window, a shiny gleaming object reflected off a metallic golden-like object on the floor under the dresser. At first I paid it no attention. Then upon second a look, it appeared to be shaped like a badge. I picked it up and that's exactly what it was. The bitch was a Fed. Shit! I should've known better. I tried calling Caine, but he didn't answer. I bounced over to his rest where he was sitting on the hood of his step-daughter's new whip.

"Why you not answering your phone?" I asked. He looked at me and blinked twice. Our warning code that five-O was in the vicinity.

"I love you, man," he said patting his heart, indicating that he was wired.

I nonchalantly observed the surroundings. I peeped the D.T. car inconspicuously acting as if they were parked waiting on someone. This was not my problem, but once again, because he was my brethren, I had to be by his side no matter what. We jumped in Tyeesha's car and sped off. Not long after they were all behind us in pursuit, Caine pulled over to the side of the road near the beach. We both hopped out with our arms spread across the hood. Cynthia, Kilaneega, and Caine's boy, Dre, jumped out with their gats cocked.

"Don't make a move, Carmello," Cynthia said closing in to pat me down. The other two assholes frisked Caine.

"What's that in your back pocket, hon?" she asked continuing to pat me down.

"Your badge, bitch!"

"That's me, but never the less, you are going to jail."

"For what? Matter of fact don't say shit else to me until my lawyer gets here."

"Good work, Caine. You delivered him as promised," Dre laughed.

"What? What you mean good work?" Caine snapped.

"Stop fronting. You said that your brother was the mastermind behind this whole thing." I knew Caine was an idiot but never a snitch or a liar.

"Don't fall into that shit, Caine. My lawyer will have us out by tonight. Y'all some real silly-ass cats. You have nothing."

"What about those New York murders?" Cynthia asked.

"Like the man said, y'all ain't got shit on us," said Caine, pulling off his wire.

"That's it," Kilaneega said. "Let's go!"

"Don't touch my body, nigga," Caine said.

"Or what?" Kilaneega asked. "You're going to kill us?"

# CHAPTER FORTY

## *Carmello*

The feds let me go and took Caine to a secret location. We were all to meet with Santiago that night. They warned me that if I tried skating on them, they'd kill my brother. They told me that my only way out of this was to give them everything I had. Deeds. Monies. Documents to properties and so forth. I was . . . we both were fucked. Stupid ass Caine. Damn. But now you see how corrupt law enforcement really is. I had no other choice but to give them what they wanted. It was the only way. But first thing was first. I had to go to Caine's house and tell Quanessa the real deal about what was going down.

"I can't believe this," she cried. "You mean all of this is from drug money? All this time Mark has been lying to me?"

"Caine," I corrected her.

"What?"

"Caine. That's his real name. I'm Carmello."

"Oh no. This shit is just too much for me. What am I supposed to tell Tyeesha?"

"Well, Quanessa, there have been enough lies, so why not just tell her the truth?"

"Just like that, Carmello? If that really is your name."

"It's my name."

"It all makes sense to me now," she said shaking her head.

"What's that?"

"Why Mark, I mean Caine, didn't want us moving to New York."

"I'm sorry you had to find out this way, Quanessa."

"You're not too sorry. I'm carrying your nephew and now his uncle and father will be behind bars for the rest of their lives."

"We're not going to jail."

"Oh? Y'all got a get-out-of-jail scam too now?" she sarcastically retorted.

"They want all the money and properties we have. Then we're free to go. But I know they're going to kill us. That's part of the reason why I'm here. I know some very important players at some banks. I'm going to give you these account numbers, so you can switch them over in your name. Everything will be untraceable. Take the money and run, sister. Please. Go on ahead to New York and live your life. And always remember, as wrong as Caine was for not telling you the truth, he loved the shit out of you and was only trying to protect y'all from his past. Everything he did since y'all got married was to keep you happy and secure."

"I don't want the dirty money, Carmello," she cried.

"Don't be foolish, Quanessa. I want my nephew to grow up in a good environment. This drug-dealing chain has to be broken. He needs to see the good things in life. He has to know that he has a choice. Tyeesha needs to know she has one too."

"God, Carmello. I feel like I'm in a bad dream and

there is no one to wake me up. Why'd you two ever get mixed up in all this bullshit?"

"My parents. The example they set opened the gate for the children to follow. Now they're dead. Our baby sister China? Gone. So you see, this is a no-win situation for us here. We knew the day would come when we'd face our demons. We never anticipated bringing any loved ones down with us, because we'd already lost what was most relevant to us."

Quanessa remained speechless. She just rocked back and forth on the white leather couch, rubbing the child inside of her.

"When am I supposed to access these accounts?" she asked through her tears.

"Get out of here by tonight. There are three plane tickets waiting for you at the airport already."

"Three tickets?"

"Yeah. Get your moms out of here too. My man Freddy will be waiting at JFK airport whenever you land. He'll set y'all up with a hotel. Two days after that you'll have all the money you need."

"Caine Carmello Jackson," she said.

"Huh?"

"The baby. It's a boy. I'm going to name him Caine Carmello Jackson."

Not wanting to upset her any further, I didn't bother telling her that the last name really was Denn. We embraced long and hard.

"I love you, sis."

"I love you too, Carmello," she responded sniffling.

# CHAPTER FORTY-ONE

## *Carmello*

After several more runs, the call from the crooked agents had finally come.

"Let me speak to my brother," I demanded.

"Hello?" Caine answered out of breath.

"You alright?"

"No. They beating the sh—"

"That's enough," Kilaneega said. "He's still alive. For now. Meet me at the Wild Diner Inn. Come alone and unarmed, Carmello. Your brother's death is just a phone call away if you try anything funny."

"Yo, be cool, man. I'm on my way."

Twenty minutes later, I arrived on the scene. The clientele was a lively bunch. I immediately scoped Kilaneega out by his signature fisherman hat and shades. He tilted his hat and walked out the side door to the waiting limousine. This was it. The showdown with Santiago. I stepped inside and the driver sped off. Kilaneega jabbed his gun under my ribcage.

"Don't make any moves, guy."

"Agent, agent, cool down. Me and Carmello are old acquaintances. Put the gun away," Santiago said. "Mello? How long has it been? Two, three years?"

"Apparently not long enough, Santiago," I responded. "Didn't I tell you no matter where you went, I'd find you?"

"So what? You want a medal or something?"

"Actually, I want your head on a stick in front of my home to ward off the evil spirits. But our humble agents of America have come up with an even better suggestion. I'll tell you all about it when we reach our destination," he said, confidently sitting back in the plush leather seating.

We arrived at a beautiful foreclosed home, where the entire block was full of houses up for sale. Santiago's three men guided me inside the home by way of gun, with Santiago and Kilaneega in tow. They were both talking shit behind my back and laughing. We walked through the living room and straight to the basement. Now the party was complete. Even Uncle Todd's punk-ass was here. Caine was badly beaten and in and out of consciousness. His right eye looked as if were about to fall out of its socket. His two top teeth were knocked out, and blood profusely poured from the corners of his mouth.

"Sit, sit, Carmello," said Santiago, pushing down on my shoulder. I sat in the wooden chair staring at Caine.

"Where's the money?" Gurthy asked.

"It's safe," I answered.

"But you're not. The deal was money first. Then your freedom."

"What? Y'all think I'm stupid or something? I give you the money, then you kill us?"

"Bastante!" Santiago said. "What is this about money? If anything, money is owed to me. Isn't that right, Caine?" He asked, smacking him out of unconsciousness.

With his eyes barely open, Caine looked up, but his head dropped back down.

"Who did this to him?" I asked.

"Isn't family just great?" Dre said looking at Uncle Todd.

"You're a real bastard, Todd," I said. "How could you turn on us like this?"

"This is a part of life, nigger. The hustle. The game. It's all about survival. You think I wanted to kill my own brother and sister-in-law? It was, and always will be, about money."

"It was you?" I yelled getting up to rush him, only to be pushed down by Santiago's men. "You were brothers man," I cried.

"Your bitch-ass daddy was a punk. We was making so much money. Then after he got rich, he was going to leave me high and dry. I helped him build Queens."

"So! You didn't have to kill him."

"That's not the only reason why I killed him. Your daddy stole your momma from me. She was supposed to be my wife. She gave birth to a child by me. I've never seen him. Y'all was supposed to be my kids. But soon as your father started making that money, your whore Momma did what she always did best. Sucked a dick for a quarter. Now look where she at."

"I'll kill you before this is over!" I screamed, with tears streaming from my eyes.

"No. I'll kill you before this is over."

"Gentlemen, this is all really touching. But there is business to discuss. I'll get straight to the point, Mello. You will always work for me, and your brother over here, well, say your goodbyes to him. He no longer of any use to me," Santiago said waving his hand.

"But you need me. And the deal is if my brother dies, then no one sees any money. Ever!"

"Carmello? You little ignorant Negro," Santiago said. "I knew you'd pull a stunt like this. That is why I am who I am." He smiled and snapped his fingers.

One of his guards set a small box on the table.

"Open it!" I stared at the box not knowing what could possibly be inside. He pulled his gun from his shoulder holster, and pointed at me.

"I said open it," he adamantly insisted. Cautiously I removed the lid of the box. My stomach twisted and I vomited, as did Uncle Todd and the agents. Inside the box were three fingers and tongues. I guess I don't have to tell you whom they belonged to? Santiago and his men laughed.

"You know, Carmello, the little one? The young girl? Oh, she was an animal. My men and I had quite a time exploring her vaginal area. She passed out so many times, I was quite sure she'd die, so I killed her. A much more painful death than the little bambina China. Then just for fun I cut the tongues and fingers of her mother and grandmother, so neither one could verbally accuse me of the crime. Or point me out in a line-up." He laughed like Satan witnessing Jesus crucified on the cross.

All I could do was sit and listen, while watching my baby brother mourn for yet another loss of loved ones.

"So, Carmello, will you now hand over those account numbers? I promise you and your brother a quick and swift death."

"Is that enough?" I asked no one in particular. Except the twenty-something undercover agents outside who had been listening in on the whole entire conversation through my wire tap since the Wild Diner Inn. They'd been watching the corrupt agents for years. Santiago was their biggest catch since who knows when? After China passed away, I was going through her things. I saw the card of Kilaneega and Detective Shudemall. Turns out that Kilaneega really meant Kill a Nigga. Shudemall was his younger protégé, looking forward to becoming the highly decorated detective he was. And I'm quite sure with more time and experience, he would. But for now he was no threat. He was just looking to be famous. I finally got the last laugh on Santiago. I laughed in his face as they led him out of the house. Gurthy, Kilaneega, and Dre looked down in shame, as the cuffs were slapped on their wrists. Uncle Todd looked at me shaking his head.

"This is how you do family?" he asked.

What occurred next happened so fast, it could not have been prevented, even if I could've stopped time. With one great big burst of energy, Caine grabbed an officer's gun from his holster and shot Uncle Todd point blank in the back of the head.

"For Mommy and Daddy!" he yelled psychotically, before being wrestled to the hard cement floor by five officers.

# CHAPTER FORTY-TWO

## *Carmello (Two Years Later)*

Due to the delicate and emotional circumstances, Caine beat the charge for killing Uncle Todd, but would be serving the rest of his natural life in prison for the murders of Starks, Silver, Chantell, Monty, Stephanie, their two daughters, and Larry. A month into his bid, he committed suicide by slitting his wrists with a razor. Now I'm all alone. I gave up everything I knew about the Decosta organization, dating way back to when my folks were working for him. He, in turn, ratted on his own father. Thus, bringing an end to the cartel. I live in California now. I'm pretty much broke. Most of my money had been confiscated by the government before it could be transferred over into Quanessa's account. What was left, went to the court fees spent on Caine before they sent him away. Caine left me a little something though. I own a home by the water in the Bay Area on the West Coast, with a boat in the yard. The game is completely out of my system. That's cool with me. No one knows me here. I'm not interested in knowing anyone, except for my new lady Tarsha, who should be here any second.

Ding! The bell rang.

Told y'all. I believe that's her right now. "Who is it?"

"Delivery for the Denn residence. Need you to sign, please." It was a Fed-Ex lady with a Valentine's day box. Shit. How could I forget? Tarsha would be tripping if I didn't get out there and get her something.

"Where do I sign at?" I asked, taking the package from her.

"Right here," she said pulling out a silencer.

Pwweet! Pwweet!

"Santiago says, 'Eat shit and die!'" she said, walking away.

# CHAPTER FORTY-THREE

## *Carmello*

I stood over the six-foot-deep empty grave with my hands clasped behind my back. The warm sunrays bore down upon my left shoulder. The black suit I wore felt as if it was absorbing all the sun's energy and was attempting to bake my soul. My mother and father stood several feet behind me.

"What's going on?" I asked.

"You fucked up," my father answered. "You fucked up real bad. I thought I taught you better than this son."

"Mello, I can't believe you let us down," my mother said shaking her head back and forth.

"Mommy, I—"

"You were supposed to protect your brother and sister."

"Caine wouldn't listen," I countered, as dark clouds began to overshadow the sun.

"You're the adult. You're no son of mine," Daddy said.

"You can't put that on me."

"You let us down, nigga," Caine accused, holding China's hand.

Rain began to fall, as they all pointed their fingers at me. I wiped the water from my face and came up with blood on my hand. It saturated my entire suit. I looked up towards the sky, as the sun reappeared as if the rain had never fallen. It got brighter and brighter, closer and closer. I blocked the blinding light with my arm.

"Carmello, can you hear me?" the unfamiliar looking man in the surgical attire asked. "Nurse, secure that oxygen mask over his mouth," he ordered, as my body began to shake uncontrollably. "He's convulsing. He's going into shock."

# CHAPTER FORTY-FOUR

## *Carmello*

*As I look up, at the sky*
*My mind starts trippin', a tear drops from my eye,*
*My body temperature falls.*
*I'm shakin,' and they breakin,' tryin' to save the Dogg.*
*Pumpin' on my chest, and I'm screamin'.*
*I stop breathin,' damn I see demons.*
*Dear God, I wonder can U save me?*
*I can't die, my Boo-Boo's 'bout to have my baby.*
*I think it's too late for prayin,' hold up;*
*A voice spoke to me and it slowly started saying.*
*—Bring your lifestyle to me I'll make it better.*
*—And how long will I live?*
*—Eternal life and forever.*
*—And will I be the G that I was?*
*—I'll make your life better than you can imagine or ever*
   *dreamed of.*
*So relax your soul, let me take control.*
*Close your eyes my son—*
*—My eyes are closed.*

My eyes fluttered open, as I lay in the hospital bed with tubes running in and out of my nose. Clear plastic wires ran through my legs and arms carrying my blood. The calendar on the wall read August 28th. Tarsha sat by my side in the yellow vinyl chair holding my hand.

"Where am I? What happened?" I asked weakly in a raspy voice. Tarsha's eyes lit up and she stood excitedly.

"Doctor!" she yelled, racing to the door. "Come quick. He's awake."

"Baby, how do you feel?" she asked crying.

"Like shit."

"Somebody tried to kill you at your house."

"Who? Why?" I asked, trying to sit up.

I don't know why I was fronting. I knew exactly who it was. I guess I just didn't want to scare her.

"Don't try to move. You've been out for a whole month."

"A month? Shit."

"Mr. Denn," the doctor said, entering the room with a small team of interns. "Welcome back. You're a very lucky man. We almost lost you."

"Well, we didn't lose him," Tarsha responded.

"How are you feeling?" Doc asked.

"Like a fucking truck hit me," I answered grimacing in pain.

"That's what happens when you get shot."

"How long am I here for?"

"I'd say at least another week. Your body needs time to heal."

I knew that if Santiago could find me way out here on the West Coast, he could find me anywhere. I had to bounce immediately. Dude's money was long and anybody could get touched if he wanted it to happen. I also knew that if he really wanted me dead, I'd be dead.

"I can't stay. I need to get out of here. Now!" I demanded, ripping the IV from my arm.

"What are you doing?" he exclaimed.

With each move I made, it hurt like shit.

"Mello, calm down," Tarsha cried, as blood spurted from the miniature puncture wound made by the needle. Doc rushed over and wrapped his hand around my arm, as one of the interns bandaged it.

"Are you crazy or something? You could bleed to death!" he yelled, applying medical tape around the bandage.

"I'll be dead if I don't get out of here." I cringed in pain as I tried to sit up.

"I can't hold you here if you don't want to stay. But it is my advice, and to your advantage, that you do. Why don't you talk it over with your girlfriend before you discharge yourself," he adamantly advised, before exiting my room with his interns following behind him.

"Why you tripping, baby? You are not in any condition to leave."

"I know who tried to get at me."

"Who?"

"Santiago."

"What? I thought he was locked up for life."

"Don't mean shit. Santiago has power."

"You sure?"

"The bitch said 'Santiago says, Eat shit and die.'"

"You not dead."

"He wants to play with me. It's his way of getting revenge for putting him away."

"But you had nothing to do with that. The Feds had been watching him."

"It doesn't matter. If we'd never hooked back up, he probably wouldn't be there. I need to get back to New York."

"And do what? If he found you here, then he'll definitely find you there."

"Help me up out this bed."

"Where are you going to go?"

"To your place for now. I've got to make some calls."

Tarsha pulled a wheelchair out from the closet, as I struggled my way off the bed to sit in it.

"Push me over to the window," I said.

"What are we looking for?" she asked, as I pulled back the curtain and looked down at the parking lot from seven floors up.

"I'll know when I see it." I scanned the comings and goings of all cars entering from the street and anyone suspiciously standing around near the vicinity of my window. Nothing appeared out of line, so I was in the clear. At least for now.

# CHAPTER FORTY-FIVE

## *Carmello*

"Cash. This is Mello. Pick up the phone," I said through Cashmere's answering machine.

"H-h-hello?" he answered groggily.

"Cash. What's up? It's me."

"Mello? It's four in the morning. What's good? Where you been at?"

"I can't talk about it right now, but I need your help."

"Yo, man, I ain't heard from you in almost three years. You gotta tell me something."

"Nigga, don't get brand new on me. I don't give a fuck how long it's been. I saved your life a while back. Now I need you to do the same for me."

"What you need, man?"

"I'll be flying in tomorrow at our regular spot. Be there to pick me up at 5:00 PM. Don't be late and don't bring nobody with you. Got it?"

"I got you, son."

"Cool."

"No doubt."

"One."

"Peace," Cashmere said hanging up the phone.

"Can you trust him?" Tarsha asked packing our suitcases.

"I don't have a choice. We go back some time though. I fed the nigga when he was starving. It's only right he pay the piper."

"There's no honor in the game, hon. You should know that better than anybody. Look how your uncle did."

"Yo, don't bring up shit you know nothing about. This is the first and last time I'll say that to you."

"Look, just because you got yourself in some shit, don't mean you got to take it out on me."

"Tarsha, maybe you should stay behind."

"Don't push me away. Let me help you."

"How are you going to help me? By getting a tombstone next to mine?"

"Don't talk like that. We'll both be alright. I promise," she said, looking into my eyes with such assuredness and sincerity that I almost believed her.

# CHAPTER FORTY-SIX

## *Carmello*

We took to the sky from San Francisco's Bay Area Airport. I pulled the shade down over my window and reclined my seat, with Tarsha's head resting on my shoulder. I thought about a lot of things while flying the friendly fucking skies. I thought about how I lost my whole family to this drug shit. It didn't matter how real you were, everything comes back to you full circle. And shit was finally making its rounds with me. I even thought back to the day when Caine first wanted to get back into this shit. I could've said no.

Now what the fuck am I supposed to do? My conscience was eating at me, but Santiago had gone way too far this time. Yeah, he killed my baby sister, but now he tried to take it a step further by killing me.

We landed at LaGuardia Airport at 5:00 PM on the dot. Cashmere was there in the 2004 SL Benz, with the trunk already open, as we exited the lobby with our suitcases. I hobbled out the double doors on crutches, still strong, carrying a duffle bag.

"God damn, nigga. What the fuck happened to you?"

Cashmere shouted out surprised, grabbing the bag off my shoulder.

"I'll tell you all about it on the way," I responded out of breath.

"This you?" he asked of Tarsha.

"Easy, daddy," she quickly responded.

"I like her already, son," he said extending his hand to her.

"Cash, Tarsha. Tarsha, Cash," I said introducing them.

I looked back through the lobby doors on some nervous shit, then stepped into the luxury car.

"So I see you back in business." I interrogated, as we rode the Van Wyck Expressway.

"Shit is going lovely," he answered, whipping past a Nissan Sentra with one hand, into the next lane.

"Oh yeah? Who you working for?"

"I'm for self. No offense. But I learned from you that ain't no money in working for a nigga." Tarsha tapped my shoulder from the backseat as the devious words escaped his lips, but I igged her.

"So you gonna tell me why you sitting on dubs?" Cashmere asked referring to my crutches.

"Santiago tried to get at me," I answered, looking out the passenger window as we passed the Gertz Mall forty minutes after leaving LaGuardia.

"Ain't he locked up?" he asked, looking out his driver's window at the weird-looking thick chick with the purple-tinted weave.

"So? He accomplished what he wanted to do. Look," I said, pulling up my shirt and showing him the unhealed incision scars on my chest.

"Holy shit!" he reacted, barely missing the blue Honda Civic ahead of him, as we passed the V.I.M. clothing store.

"Be careful," Tarsha warned Cashmere, nervously holding onto my headrest.

"I got this, Miss. I been doing this for years."

"Mello?" she called expecting me to say something.

"Relax, baby," I coolly responded.

"The streets is missing you, Mello," Cashmere said out of nowhere.

"Oh yeah? How so?"

"Niggas is out here getting the two-eleven put on them ev'yday. Not to bring up old shit, but when you and Caine was out here shit was right."

"I'm done with it. I just need a place to lay low for a minute until I figure out my next move."

"I got you, my dude. You know you my nigga," he said with a wide but suspect smirk on his grill.

# CHAPTER FORTY-SEVEN

## *Carmello*

After living in Florida and Cali, I forgot how cold it could get back home in New York. It was the middle of October and the temperature turned frigid our first week there.

Against my better judgment in fashion, Tarsha insisted on copping us matching Phat Farm leather snorkels from Harlem. It was cool though. She loved doing shit for me. I thought everything was going to be alright. I still had money in the bank and was going to stay legit no matter what. After losing everything, I'd at least have my self-respect. All this money Cashmere was making had did him some real criminal justice. He owned three houses out in Corona, Queens, a store which he rented out to a poppy on 204<sup>th</sup> and Linden Boulevard, and a limo service. He lived out in Maspeth, Long Island.

His house had the *Leave It To Beaver* landscape effect in front of the five-bedroom home. Six steps led up to the double doors, with grayish marble columns supporting the white-shingled awning. As we pulled into the driveway, a purple 2007 jaguar sped in past us, and stopped inches before the three-car garage.

Kelis's hit single "I'm Bossy" demanded respect, as its bass-enthralled rhythm rattled the windows of Cashmere's sexy accountant's luxury ride. She rolled the windows up and stepped out one foot at a time. Cashmere pulled up behind her.

"That's you?" I asked.

"She's my accountant slash deep-throat specialist. Pardon my French, ma," he apologized looking back at Tarsha.

"Whatever. You not talking about me."

"I like this girl," he smiled, pointing back at her with that devious smirk.

We all stepped out the car as he walked up to his accountant and blessed her with a kiss that made her eyes cross.

"Somebody's happy to see me," she said pecking his lips after the kiss to a prelude.

"You handled that?" he asked.

"In the trunk," she answered, nodding her head towards the rear of the car.

"Toss me the keys."

He grabbed two leather, brown duffel bags and handed one to her.

"Go get the door," he said, staying two steps behind her, with us in tow. He took a look back then let us walk by him before walking inside the house. He tossed the bags on the couch. He quickly disarmed the alarm by pressing a sequence of numbers on the keypad, on the wall by the left door. I was impressed by the expensive layout of his place. No doubt in my mind that his new ho had decorated it.

"You like my come up, my nigz?" he asked walking towards the bar.

"You are too rude, Cash," said the accountant.

"What you talking about?"

"Anyway. Hi. I'm Lexi," she said pulling off her coat. "You'll have to excuse him for his manners. I haven't got him all the way trained yet," she said looking over at him as she removed her coat. "You must be—"

"Carmello," I answered before she could finish her sentence. "This is my lady, Tarsha."

"Hi," Tarsha said.

"Nice to meet you."

"Same here," she answered, also removing her coat.

"Let me get those," Lexi said, taking our coats and placing them in the closet down the hallway. Her high-heels click-clacked and echoed off the hardwood floor and walls.

"Sit down, man. You making me feel tired standing there on them crutches. What y'all drinking?" He dropped three ice cubes apiece in four glasses.

"Water's good. I can't be drinking fucked up like this."

"How 'bout you, Tanya?"

"Tarsha," she corrected him. "I'm good with water also."

"More for me," he said, filling his glass with some Paul Mason.

"You look like you gained a li'l weight, son," I said.

"A nigga eating now. Know what I'm saying?" He patted his used-to-be-toned stomach, now hanging over his waistline.

"Can I use your bathroom?" Tarsha asked.

"Right down the hallway to your right."

As she walked through the hallway, Lexi passed her on the way back to the living room.

"How long are you two in town for?" she asked me.

"For a minute. So what you doing with this knuckle-head?"

"Oh a little bit of this. A little bit of that."

"Yeah, man. I done found me something good. Baby, how many languages you speak?"

"Four! French, Spanish, Italian, and Japanese."

"Drop him the hellos," Cashmere bragged.

"Bonjour, hola, ciao, konichiwa."

"Like I said, what you doing with him?"

"Don't be no hater, playa. You got yourself a nice li'l something too."

"She's very pretty," Lexi complimented.

"You got somewhere we can talk, Cash? This is some serious business," I said.

"Lexi, how about when Tarsha comes out the bathroom, you give her a tour of the castle so me and Mello can kick it for a minute?"

"I think I can manage that. She can help me get dinner started."

"So what's on your mind homie?" Before I could respond, his cell rang.

"Yo, what's up?" he answered. "Yeah I will."

He walked back towards the bar and poured himself another drink. "Uh-huh. Just like you said, dukes. Uh-huh. Oh no doubt. Trust me. I got you. Ol' boy got it coming. Look yo. I got some company from out of town right now, so I'm kind of busy. Hit me back later on that. Lexi is fine. Oh yeah. Come on, man," he smirked. "She's just my accountant. Hello? Hello?" he said looking down at the phone. "Damn. These niggas wit' these cell phones. Calls be dropping all the time. Anyway where was we at?"

"I need a place to lay low."

"Son, I told you I got you. You need some money or something?"

"Naw. I'm good on that. I'm still spending small faces," I lied.

"Oh yeah. I forgot who I was talking to. Hey man, listen! I heard what happened to Caine while he was locked up. That's some real fucked-up shit. I never thought he'd go out like that."

"Caine was a warrior. I don't believe for a damn second that he killed himself. It's bullshit. But even if he did, he made fools out of the feds. He killed niggas they couldn't even touch. He went out the way he would've wanted to. On his own terms."

"Still though—" he said sipping from the glass.

"Look. That's enough about my brother, alright? So tell me something, Cash, how in the fuck you come up with all this money?"

# CHAPTER FORTY-EIGHT

## *Carmello*

After one day back in the NYC, Cash showed me just how he came into all his doe. He'd taken my place. Same position, just a different player. The dumb nigga. I guess he didn't learn shit from me and my fam's mistakes. What made it even more fucked up was he wasn't working for Santiago. He was working for his father's brother, Manuel Decosta. And that shit made me wonder if I had to start watching this nigga. I mean Cash was always straight with me. If he thought I was being set up, I know he'd put a dude on.

We rode through the streets of Southside, Jamaica in his black Denali, sitting on twenty-fours. He was really feeling himself and so was the hood, and niggas treated me as if I'd never done this before. I was just another dick riding in the passenger seat of a baller playing at home. I ain't never felt so alone. Plus my cellular phone was on roam. No contacts. No rep. No respect. What the fuck yo? But my paper was still long as the days of thunder. I could still make bird-niggas feel the wrath of the hummer. And if this nigga ever tried to front on me, I had no problem putting two in back of his head. Because at the end of the day, guess what? I was still Carmello.

After doing his nightly round of pick-ups and deliveries, Cash and I headed out to a bar in Patterson, New Jersey. When we walked through the doors, he was treated like a superstar. The bouncers gave him dap. All the waitresses pressed him with hugs and kisses, while he sipped from glasses they carried on their serving trays. As for me, all I received was stares of betrayal and rehearsed glares of contemptuous disdain. We stepped to the VIP section and sat on the couch closest to the emergency exit. I'd taught ol' boy well. Always sit nearest to the exit in the event you got to bounce in a hurry.

"I know I been gone for a minute, mayne, but why all these cats keep looking at me sideways?" I asked him.

Fifty and Mobb Deep's song sliced into our conversation, and the crowd around us started going crazy.

"I have no idea, yo. Don't wet it though. You rolling with the Cash. You be a'ight."

"Mmm, is that right?"

"Fo' sho, my nizzle. You want a drink man?"

"Gin and juice."

"You still on that Snoop Dogg shit?"

"I can't afford to be off-point in my condition. I'm a month out the hospital, B."

"I hear ya. But a nigga like me is gonna get his swerve on." He signaled a gorgeous waitress over and placed the two orders. My drink, and a Belvedere on the rocks for himself. He pulled out a wad of hundreds and spread them out across the table.

"So tell me more about this Manuel?"

"Not really much to tell. He's Santiago's uncle and he running the show now."

"Yeah, but how in the hell did you get hooked up with him?"

"What's up, Mello? You a li'l green behind the ears or something?"

"Never that. I'm just wondering why you acting like I'm new to this?"

"You may as well be. You been gone for two years, then expect it to be all love when you pop the fuck back up, out of thin air."

"Nigga, I was trying to change my life and do the right thing."

"What the fuck is the right thing, dawg? Slaving from nine-to-five for them crackers?"

"The right thing is not doing this bullshit here no more!" I responded, raising my voice and lifting the crutch on my right.

"The right thing, huh?" he chuckled. "Was you thinking about the right thing when you was treating me like a sucker?"

"What are you talking about?"

"The day when you kicked me to the fucking curb when the spot got robbed. Remember that shit?"

"I was trying to save your life my dude. That shit was never for you and it still isn't."

"Not for me? You the one all shot the fuck up."

"Nigga my entire family is dead behind this shit. If I would've put a stop to this back then, Caine and China would still be here."

"Oh. That's why you clowned me? Because you cared so much about my life. Then why the fuck you put me on in the first place?"

"You wanted to make some doe and you was from the block. We grew up together. I was looking out for my dawg."

"You was looking out for yourself. That li'l bit of doe you was giving me wasn't paying the bills. But it's okay. I'm wit' that right muthafucka now. And nobody gives me flack. I got the block sewed the fuck up. They ain't trying to hurt nothing."

"They?"

"Him," he corrected himself. "Manuel."

"You said they."

"Manuel, nigga. He taking care of the god. You saw the rib."

"All I'm saying is be easy, dukes. You don't know about this shit."

"What? I done smoked plenty of niggas over this shit. My résumé is long. If you don't believe me, just ask about me. I got something I never had rolling with you."

"Oh yeah? What's that?" I asked sipping my drink as soon as the waitress passed it to me.

"Money," he answered, passing the waitress a fifty dollar tip, as she placed his drink before him. "Power," he stated slapping her ass. "And respect from each and everyone of these crumb-ass niggas in this bitch." He tossed back his drink and slammed the glass on the table.

"That's all good, but at the end of the day is it worth your life?" He looked around the club ingesting the provocative dancing of the half-naked women and the dick riding niggas that had his back, then stared me directly in the eyes with a smirk.

"Yeah," he answered.

"Whatever, man."

"Is that my nigga Carmello?" said the unfamiliar face to my left. I looked up and nodded.

"I know you?" I asked.

"Oh yeah, fam, we goes way back."

"Naw, man, I don't think you know me."

"I used to kick it with your brother. We was like this," he said crossing his fingers.

"I don't know you, man. And since I don't know you, why don't you step, son."

"You heard that man, nigga, bounce!" Cash ordered standing up.

The dude held his hands up and stepped back easily.

"Easy, playa, I ain't looking for no trouble."

"Yeah I know you not," Cash said pulling his jacket to the side, revealing his holster.

"Alright. Chill. Yo, Mello. I'ma see you my dude. Peace," the stranger said walking away.

"He anybody you know?" Cash asked.

"Not at all."

"Then fuck him. You rolling wit' the Cash, baby. I'm gonna order me another drink. You want something else besides that West Coast shit you sipping?"

"You can get me a vodka and cranberry. I'm going to take a piss, man. I'll be right back."

I hobbled my ass to the bathroom and stood one of my crutches against the marble stall, using the other to maintain my balance. After pissing, I placed my hands near the sensor at the sink and washed them, as the bathroom door slowly opened and in walked the stranger.

"Melly-Mel," he said knocking my crutch down away from the stall. I reached for my gun, but he was quicker.

"Don't even do it to yourself, playa. Just toss that shit over here. It ain't even that serious," he warned, aiming. I slowly extended my hand towards him.

"Naw, playa. Put it on the floor and kick it over here." I knelt down as far as the increasing pain in my body would allow, and placed it on the floor, kicking it over to him. He picked it up and pulled out the clip then checked the chamber.

"You slipping, dawg. You don't even keep one in the

chamber?" All I could do was stand there. The crazy shit was that if he was going to pop me, I wasn't afraid. At least now I could be with my family.

"You still try'na figure out who I am, right?"

"I don't give a shit who you are. If you was going to use that, I'd already be dead."

"You still a fucking psychologist, huh?"

"Naw, nigga. I'm still Carmello. You gonna shoot? Shoot, nigga. Think I'm afraid to die?"

"Yo, Mello, what the fuck? You fall in?" Cash asked walking into the bathroom with his drink in hand. The stranger quickly spun around and aimed at him.

"Join the party homie," he said.

"You making a big mistake, yo." Cash said standing next to me with his hands raised.

"A mistake? Naw, nigga, I ain't making no mistake." He locked the bathroom door to hinder any more unexpected visitors from entering.

"Ain't you that fool from earlier? Man what the fuck this all about?" Cash asked.

"Your man. Your man right here. This bitch-ass nigga!" he yelled aiming at me again. The bathroom door exploded off its hinges and three huge bouncers charged through the door, before he could react and hopped on his head. The biggest bouncer twisted his arm and the gun dropped to the floor, causing it to go off. *Oh shit, not again.*

"Get the fuck up," the bouncer said, scooping the stranger off the floor and slamming him against the cold and hard marble wall.

"Hold up, Big Boy," Cash said walking up to the would-be killer. "Who the fuck are you?"

"You better answer real quick and real right," said Big Boy.

I leaned against the nearest wall and picked up my crutch. When ol' boy didn't give them the appropriate answers, a serious case of the ass-whoopings began to materialize. No one held back. Not even Cash. As the bouncers caught wreck upon his grill, Cash repeatedly rammed his knee up into his jewels. I hadn't heard screams like that since the days of Santiago and his peoples punishing betrayers and enemies.

"You want some of this, Mello?" Cash said turning around briefly. Half the club was staring through the bathroom's entrance cheering and laughing while dude got his ass handed to him. For an instant, dude even looked at me as if to say, "Get'em off me! Can't you see them? They're all over me." But fuck that. Why should I have been feeling sorry for him? Two seconds ago, he was ready to put a cap in my ass.

At the same time I couldn't seem to bypass the vague familiarity in his face. Then again, it was probably more of the feeling of never wanting to be in the fucked-up predicament he was in right now. When they finally finished beating his ass, he dropped to the floor, landing in the fetal position. It almost appeared as if everything began to move in slow motion. Even Cash talking sounded like chopped and screwed music.

"See, Mello, there's a new sheriff in town." He gave Big Boy and the other two bouncers a dap, and kicked the moaning, damn-near crippled, stranger in the face.

# CHAPTER FORTY-NINE

## *Santiago*

"So you looking forward to getting out of here soon?" Skelly asked.

"I am ready to go home. American prison is bullshit. In my country they consider this vacation."

Skelly was Santiago's cellmate who was doing a thirty-year bid for a bank robbery gone awry. He and Santiago had become quite fond of one another's entrepreneurial vision. They were both about money no matter how extreme the circumstances it took to get paper. Skelly, who was thirty years old, had gotten knocked two years ago with his partner in crime, Enoch—a young, wild muthafucka who didn't know who his father was until he was killed four years ago. When Skelly met Enoch, he took him under his wing after running away from a group home in Florida when he was just fifteen. He saw that gangsta potential in him and knew that, because he had no family, he could easily be persuaded into doing his bidding. And he was right. They robbed banks all across the states for five years until Skelly's unfortunate capture. Instead of leaving the bank in the five minutes as they had always done, Enoch decided he was going to go back for more money. That extra two minutes was more than enough for time the S.W.A.T. team to shoot Skelly in the ankle, as he ran behind Enoch pushing him up the street to the awaiting green SUV.

"Just go, kid. I'll be a'ight. Go!" Skelly yelled, lying on the ground, holding his ankle with the stolen money spread out all around him. He laughed when they surrounded him with their weapons pointed at him. He stopped laughing when they all tazed his black-ass. Enoch hopped inside the sports utility van and the driver dipped off into the traffic. That day the cops beat the shit out of Skelly but he never turned over any information about Enoch. Not once did he ever regret his decision to take the fall for both of them. He always understood that he'd never see his li'l man again. After leaving la-la land, Skelly returned to reality.

"This'd be a vacation, huh?" he said dipping a piece of bread into turkey gravy inside the metal lunch-tray.

"Si. Where I from you no luxury of eating lunch when in prison. No quality food that is. You know?"

"I feel you. So what the fuck you gonna do when you get out? I know one thing for sho', you won't be starving for a fucking thing. You the smoothest dresser in this entire place. You did four years out of a lifetime sentence. That's gangsta money," Skelly concluded, placing the four-hundred-pound weight back between the holds of the bench.

"No gangsta. It is that businessman money. When I get out of here there is much to do. Oh yes. Very much."

"You must got yourself one hell of a lawyer on retainer?"

"A good lawyer is only part of it. When you have money to make bright Christmas or good summer for judge, you can beat just about any case."

"So look here, man. I know you got mad connections on the outside. When you hit them streets again get word out to my boy to holla at me. I'll give you his picture when we get back to the tier."

"For you, it is not a problem. I will not even charge you a fee."

"Well that's real good looking out, Santiago."

"Decosta. You got a visitor," the correction officer yelled through the rusting steel bars. Two more guards arrived at either side of him.

"I holla at you lata, Santz. Go handle your B.I." Santiago walked down the long hallway unshackled, but closely guarded by the officers. They weren't worried about him trying to escape. It was for his *own* safety. See over the many years of dealing, he'd crossed many lines and cut the throats of just about everybody in the game. So his enemies ranged from far and vast. At any time or turn, he could've, better yet should've, been stuck like the pig he was.

"Gentlemen. Who is it that is here for Santiago?" he said, as they neared the visiting room personally designated for him only. The officers said nothing until they got to the room.

"Sit down. Your visitor will be here in a moment," commanded the veteran correctional officer.

Santiago sat in the wooden chair crossing one leg over the other in that unusual feminine-styled way he'd been doing since his teenage years. Accompanied by two other correctional officers, Manuel Decosta entered the large room sporting an Italian custom tailored tan Coragliotti wool and cashmere pinstriped suit. He was average height and slender, with a receding hairline slicked back into a ponytail. A distracting black mole stood out on his left cheek, with hair growing out of it. He opened his arms to embrace his nephew, whom he hadn't seen since the days of Colombia when he was just a chico, trying to be a man.

"Uncle. What a surprise. You are here much earlier than your letter indicated," Santiago said, still grasping his uncle's hand as they sat opposite one another.

"You look well, sobrino. You've been taking care of yourself?"

"Si, Uncle."

"No lucha?"(fight)

"They don't dare."

"Very well then."

"What has my lawyer said? When can I come home?"

"Just a little longer. It is not as simple as we thought it would be. But we are looking for a release next month."

"I am looking forward to seeing my family. How is my poppa?"

"He is well."

"Is he still upset with me?"

"We speak on that later. The important thing first is to get you out of this hell."

"Is Mr. Cashmere doing the thing correctly?"

"That is of no concern to you. I have a question."

"Anything Uncle."

"I want you to be honrado."

"Si, of course."

"I hear through the wire that you tried to have Carmello Junior assassinated. Is this true?" Santiago looked him directly in the eyes and lied.

"Uncle, I have bigger things to concern myself with, than some dumb nigger on the outside."

"I'm going to leave now. I have to get back home. I will be back in a month. That is when you be ready to go from here."

They both rose to their feet, embraced, and kissed one another's cheek. Manuel held both sides of Santiago's face and kissed his lips.

"I am ready," Manuel said to the guards. Two guards escorted him in one direction, and three more took Santiago in the other. Santiago turned around and watched his uncle walk down the long hallway until he was out of his sight.

"Let's go, Decosta," the stocky C.O. said.

# CHAPTER FIFTY

## *Carmello*

"Baby, I want you to go back home," I said to Tarsha, sitting at a table in the OG restaurant, waiting on our order.

"I've hardly seen you since we've been here. Now you want me to leave? I'm trying to be here for you."

"That's all cool, but you don't belong here. This is my problem. There's a lot you don't know about me and, regrettably enough, I owe some retribution. I can't get you involved with this bullshit."

"I'm not scared, Carmello."

"That has nothing to do with it. I've lost so much getting other people caught up in my shit. I can't go through it anymore."

"Everybody who stood by you wanted to be there, I'm sure."

"I'm not going to argue with you about this."

"Me neither," she said folding her arms.

"Damn it, Tarsha. Why do you have to be so stubborn? Don't you see I'm not about shit? You see the kind of people I deal with."

"Please, Mello. You act like you the first dude I ever met that was hood. You trying to save my life, but can't even save your own."

"That's fucked up."

"You're right. I'm sorry. I shouldn't have said that. Come here," she said kissing my lips. "But I'm still not leaving."

"You's about a stubborn ass."

"You best to believe it," she said, sipping her bottle of carrot juice.

"So there's no way I'ma convince you to go back home?"

"No way. I'm riding with Mello til' death do us part."

"What about everything you have back at home? Your job. Your family. I mean, you can't just turn away from that."

"I know you'd never intentionally endanger my life babe, so I'm with you."

"But why would you put yourself out here on front street when you know people are trying to kill me?"

"I don't know."

"That's the problem. I think that this shit is a rush for you. It's exciting."

"I'm not into excitement, I'm into you. What I'm trying to figure out though is, what made you run all the way back out here? The man found you in Cali. I don't trust your boy and I don't think you do either. So what's the real reason you're here? And don't bullshit me, Mello. Let me get a straight answer."

# CHAPTER FIFTY-ONE

## *Cashmere*

"Lexi? You finished wit' dem books yet?" I asked her.

"Just about. You're lucky I feel for you. It wasn't easy. I was up since 3:00 in the morning doing this. What time is Manuel coming to pick up his money?"

"He's pulling in front of the house right now."

I opened the door before he could ring the bell. He was alone as usual. He never traveled with security. I respected that about him.

"Cash," he said walking right in after I opened the door. "You have something for me?"

"No doubt. Baby, get the man his shit." Lexi walked to the back and returned with a briefcase. She placed it on the table and popped it open. He lifted a stack of hundreds from it and visually calculated the rest of the contents inside.

"Hermoso, where is this Carmello? You said he'd be here."

"That nigga was supposed to be here. He been gone all day."

"You fucking with me? You know how I feel about lying."

"You know I don't be fronting, right, babe?" I said looking at Lexi.

"No. He's been in and out ever since he's been here. I believe he's out with his girlfriend."

"He is not by himself?"

"Naw, man. He flew out with some bitch."

"Contain your offensive linguistic content before the woman."

"Thank you, Manuel," she said.

"You want me to call his cell?" I asked.

"No. I want you to call me the instant he walks through the door."

"Okay. So we good?" I asked nodding towards the money.

"Very good. I shall return later this evening with more product for you," he said closing the case.

"What time, man? The workers are hungry out there."

"As they say in your country, 'Don't worry, I got you!'"

"A'ight, yo. One."

"I don't trust him, baby," Lexi said.

"Don't matter. Only thing I trust is that gwop."

"I mean, it doesn't strike you as odd as to why he's so interested in meeting up with Carmello?"

"He wants to kill him. Shit. That nigga a snitch. You know that. He got the whole hood looking at him suspect."

"And you riding around with him like it's nothing. What's up with that?"

"Trust me, Lexi, I got big plans. Major shit is about to go down and you and I are about to come off on top."

"You turn me on when you talk like that."

"You know how I do?"

"I know, baby. I'm about to take a shower. You coming to join me?"

"Fo' sho," I said, smacking her ass as she walked away.

Lexi was alright. She handled my day to day and was a hell of a good fuck. Shit. I'm lying. She was an excellent fuck. She was a good girl. Manuel hired her as an accountant for me back when. We hit it off just like that and been doing the damn thang ever since. But then, there were those times when she did work for Manuel and would be gone for days at a time. Didn't matter none though. When she wasn't around, I always kept something on stand by. Shit. Carmello thought he was the man at one time. I'm glad his ass is back to see me doing big things. Sky's the limit. And if Manuel try to flip the script on me, I got one hundred and twelve ways to simmer or sauté his red-beans-and-rice-eating ass. Fucker!

Me and Lexi drove into Rosedale and parked at J&S pizza for a slice of that Sicilian shit.

"I'm just gonna run in and get that shit, baby. What you want on yours?"

"Pepperoni with extra cheese," she said.

"A'ight. I'll be right back."

"Let me get a small box of Sicilian with pepperoni," I said to the owner Tommy.

"Hey Cash. What the dealy-o, homeboy?"

"Chilling. How long that gonna take?"

"The usual. About ten minutes. You got your lady in the car?"

"You know it. Make sure there's extra cheese on that shit, man. Y'all be flaking with the shit."

"Ay, don't I always do you right?"

"Whatever, nigga."

He threw the rectangular pie into the oven and slammed it shut.

"You got anything new for me, Cash?" he asked squeezing his nose and sniffing.

"Yeah. I got you, Tommy. What you need?"

"Let's see. Friday night? I got a c-note."

"A'ight. Let me run out to the car. You working me, Tommy-Tom."

"Fuck it. I'm putting money in your pocket."

"True that. Be right back," I said walking back out to the car.

"Lexi, pass me one of those thangs out the arm rest."

"What's up, baby, Tommy want something?"

"Yep. You know he stay thirsting for that soda."

"Yo, Cashmere!" I heard somebody shout from across the street at the Rosedale Lanes bowling alley. It was dark and I really couldn't make out the face or shape. But just like a fool, I waited for him to cross through the two-way traffic with one hand in his pocket.

"Baby. Hurry up and pass me my shit." I held it close to my side, behind my leg. As he reached my side of the street, he took a cigarette from his pocket and lit it. Soon as his face hit the light I already knew who it was, and I hoped that this nigga wasn't gonna make me have to give him a sleeping pill.

"What's up?" he asked puffing the cigarette hard.

"Yo. I hope you not here for trouble. Less you wanna die tonight?"

"I'm not dying tonight. You better look across that street." I struggled to see in the dark, but did make out five dudes on standby in the lot watching his back.

"Yeah," he chuckled. "So be easy and put that shit away. I'm not here for beef."

"Naw. I'm good," I said still looking at his peoples over his shoulder. "Speak your piece."

"You and your li'l crew did me real durty. But that's alright. It's not you I got the problem with."

"You got beef with my man, you got beef with me."

"What if I told you that I have a business proposal for

you? Business that can get you up from under Manuel. Think you living the life now?"

"I'm listening. First tell me what the beef is between you and my boy. Then tell me what you know about Manuel."

"No time for that now. I got a game going on inside. Money on the line, feel me? But you call this number tomorrow and we can link up."

"How I know you not setting me up?"

"Setting you up for what? Everybody knows that all those properties you own is Manuel's, including that bitch in the whip. So stop stunting, nigga. Do we have a deal?" he asked holding out his hand for a pound.

"Too slow," he laughed, as I went to give him a dap. He walked back across the street with much more confidence than he did when he ran over.

"Who was that, baby?" Lexi asked

"An old friend," I answered walking inside to get the pizza. When I walked back out, Lexi was quickly hanging up her phone.

"We need to get home. I have to be to work early."

"Yeah? Manhattan or Manuel?" I asked reversing into the oncoming traffic.

# CHAPTER FIFTY-TWO

## *Carmello*

Since Tarsha had never been to New York, I decided to give her the full-fledged tour, starting with my old hood. Cash wasn't helping me any and I was beginning to suspect that he was up to some shady shit. Me and Tarsha decided to get us a room at the Howard Johnson hotel on Long Island. We rented a car and drove until we reached our destination; I hadn't been, in quite some time, to visit the cemetery where my parents and siblings rested.

"This is it," I said, stopping in front of the four tombstones lined up a foot apart from one another. "I haven't been here since my sister died," I confessed. I knelt down and placed a rose by China's picture.

"Y'all must've been really close?" Tarsha assumed.

"We were more than close. Words can't even begin to explain."

"What's this right here?" she asked, standing in front of the tombstone with no inscription, except for a birth date.

I looked up towards the sky and then to her, as if to insinuate that she already knew.

"Oh no, Carmello. Tell me that's not what I think it is?"

"What do you think it is?"

"Is that for you?"

I looked at her again with a blank expression.

"Mello, is that tombstone yours?"

"Yeah."

"Why? How could you be so insensitive? What makes you think I want to see something like this?"

"You wanted to know me. This is what I know right here, Tarsha, death. You know what that is? Death. This is my life. All right here under the earth."

"You're crazy. Do you think you're the only one who's ever lost somebody you loved? Hello! Wake up, Mello. The world doesn't revolve around just you. I lost both my parents in a car accident when I was three. Did you forget where I come from? L.A. West Coast. Compton. My brother was shot down right in front of me. So don't stand there and act like I ain't been through shit too. You don't see me out here with my own tombstone stuck in the ground, feeling all sorry for myself."

"Know what the difference is, Tarsha? You lost everything while you were a little girl."

"That doesn't mean anything. People die everyday. Oh well. Boo-hoo. Get over it."

"If it's that easy for you to get over your dead family, then maybe you might be with the wrong dude. This is my family right here, and I'll never be over it until the day I die."

"Hence," she said waving her hand across all the gravesites.

"I brought you here because I thought we were really getting close. Maybe I was wrong?"

"What's going on up here?" she asked pointing to my head.

"It's not what's going on up here," I said, catching her

hand. "It's about what's going on down here." I redirected her hand to my heart. "Who do I have now?"

"You have me," she said hugging me. "You have to beat this morbid state of mind, alright? Yes you almost lost your life, but guess what? You still here, babe. We can get out the state, even out the country. You don't have to stay here looking for Santiago, or chill with that snake, Cashmere. They're not the reason you're here. You came back to New York to die, didn't you?"

"I came back to be with my family. My brother and sister wouldn't be here if it wasn't for me."

"Nothing's going to bring them back. So where do you go from here?"

"I don't know."

"So will you please let me help you?" she asked taking my hand.

Snow flurries began to fall, as we stood atop the hill. She pulled down on my hand and kissed me.

"Mello, will you let me help you get through this? Please," she begged.

"No, go back home," I said heartlessly, jerking my hand out of her loving grasp. "It's not going to be safe out here for you once word is out that I'm really back, and if I know Cashmere, he's already told everybody. You have to remember one thing, Tarsha?"

"What's that?" she asked, crying with her back turned to me.

"In these niggas' minds I left New York as a snitch."

Back at the hotel I'd finally convinced Tarsha to go back home, under the condition that I'd be back to marry her.

"You know you're my world," I assured her as we lay in bed.

"I know."

"Yeah. You know everything," I chuckled.

We turned to one another and pecked before kissing deeply. She cried as the kissing intensified, becoming much more meaningful with every breath. She placed her hand around the back of my neck and kissed me even deeper.

"Oh God, I don't want to leave you," she said.

"Shh." I began softly kissing her entire body. I placed my fingers between hers and entered her love. As I carefully stroked in and out of her, she pushed back, seductive and eager. It was hot. It was soft. It was the best lovemaking we ever had. And for a moment, I almost wanted to go back home with her. But my place was here. No matter how much I cared for her.

"This is the end of the Denn saga, baby," I whispered in her ear.

She cried still harder. "Please stop saying that," she wept.

It was 7:00 when I woke up. The rising sun managed to peek through the dark curtains in front of the patio-styled doors of the balcony. I went to kiss Tarsha one last time before we said goodbye, but she was already gone.

# CHAPTER FIFTY-THREE

## *Carmello*

"Who the fuck is it?" Cashmere yelled opening the front door.

"Carmello." Soon as Cash opened the door, I forced my way in and hopped on him.

"What the hell are you doing, man?" he yelled, falling on the floor with me on top of him.

"Tell me what the fuck is going on, Cash. You been acting funny ever since I got here."

"Get the fuck off of him," Lexi said coming up from behind me with the hammer to the back of my head.

"What the fuck is going on, Cash?" I asked again.

"Think I won't pop you? I said get off him," Lexi repeated cocking it this time.

"Chill, baby. It's a'ight," Cash said holding his hands up to her. She steady stayed focused on getting me off him. I raised up and took a step back.

"Easy, baby," he said grabbing the gun out her hand by the head. "What's up with you man? You looking to get popped? Lexi don't play."

"Neither do I. I been out in the street today, nigga. You ain't been real with me."

"What you talking about?"

"I was up in the barber shop today. You ain't been telling me everything, yo."

"I don't know what you talking about, Mello."

A knock at the door broke the monotony. I took a step back.

"Hold up, man," he said opening the door.

"Hola." I automatically knew this was the infamous Manuel, dressed suave like Santiago used to dress with a fancy car outside. He smelled like money.

"Are you going to let me in or do you think I just want to stand outside, Cash?" he asked.

"My bad. Yeah. Come on in. This my man M—"

"Carmello Jr. Si? Lexi." He gave Lexi a nice long kiss and she obliged by kissing him back.

"Alright. That's enough," Cashmere said getting hot.

"Carmello, it is such a pleasure to finally meet your acquaintance after all the good things I've heard about you." All I could do was stand there looking back and forth between him and Cash. Now I was really bugging.

"Aren't you going to say anything?" he asked smiling.

"What am I supposed to say, man? I don't know you."

"We're all family, man," he said slapping my shoulder.

"Naw. You ain't no family of mine. I don't got no family."

"I've been asking about you. Cash told me you were flying in. You're a difficult individual to catch."

"What you been looking for me for? I owe you some money?"

"Chill, Mello," Cash said.

"You don't say shit to me, funny-style muthafucka."

"Calm down, Mello. I want you to know that the past

is the past. What is done is done. Capeesh? I have no qualms with you."

"Okay. So I know that's not the reason why you been looking for me. So what you want?"

"I have a business proposition for you. Are you interested?"

"I don't even know you, man."

"Then I am out the door," he said preparing to bounce.

"Hold up," I said walking out with him to his car.

"How'd you know I was here?"

"Your buddy informed me the night you called."

"Did he?"

"Care to take a ride out to Whitestone with me? We can talk more on the way."

"What's in Whitestone?"

"Opportunity." He stepped into the driver's seat. I hesitated to get in.

"What do you fear? Here," he said placing his gun on the passenger seat. "It is loaded. You feel fear, then use it." I looked back at the front door. Cash was still wiping the blood off his lip from me snuffing him.

"Let's ride," I said getting in. I cocked the shit and held it in my lap as he backed out the driveway.

"It is finally good to meet with you. I also knew your father. I am sorry to hear of your recent tragedies."

"So am I."

"How are you doing with money?"

"I'm good."

"You do not look like it. You are not the man I've heard so much about."

"Start talking, man. I don't like wasting my time."

"Santiago is coming home."

"So."

"He is very upset with you."

"I know that," I said pulling up my shirt.

"So he did do that to you?"

"Who else?"

"How do you know this?"

"Because the bitch who did it said 'Santiago says eat shit and die!'" I yelled.

As we crossed the bridge into Whitestone, I looked out the window at the tugboat carrying garbage. The seagulls were spread about, congregating atop the piles of debris and recyclables. Even though it was brick outside, I had the window cracked and could hear them singing the eerie songs of deprived hunger. The sea scavengers furiously flapped their wings and pecked at one another, trying to protect their necks as they fought over the empty cans of soda.

"He was told to let it go. His father will not be pleased."

"So what is this business proposition thing about?"

"I'll get right to the point. I want you to work for me. I've already discussed the matter over with my brother. That is it. Are you in, or, are you out?"

Damn, here I was fucked again. I could go back to Cali and finish up with school, marry Tarsha, and start a family. But then I'd be looking over my shoulder for the rest of my life. I couldn't watch my back and hers at the same time everyday. And if I lost one more person because of my bullshit, I'd probably kill myself.

"Why me, yo? You got Cash."

"Do you really believe I take him seriously?" He laughed. "Why do you think I have Lexi as his accountant? The fool. He is ignorant."

"Why are you using him then?"

"Because the street knows him, but fears me. I feel in time though he will become a snitch. I do not trust him."

"But you trust me?"

"I trust that you have the ability to move product a lot faster than he. Why should I trust him, when he's the one who told me you were here. Isn't he your friend? Let me put this money back in your pocket. Santiago's day is over. He will pay for his insubordination. Prison was way too kind to him. What is it you would like to do to him when he comes home?"

"You're asking me?"

"What would you like for me to do the man, my nephew, who has taken your entire family from you? Better yet, what is it you would like to do?"

"What can I do?"

"Whatever you want, Carmello. I personally would be wanting a little revenge." He smiled, turning into the circular driveway of his mini-mansion.

# CHAPTER FIFTY-FOUR

## *Cashmere*

Suddenly I wasn't trusting Mello no more. I thought Manuel wanted to kill his ass, or wanted to set him up to go up North or something like that. Shit. How wrong I was. Manuel wanted this fool back on payroll. How in the world dude send your family to prison and you cool with that? I was fucking fuming. Ol' bitch-ass nigga. I wasn't even try'na hear that. No way, no how. He was not going to ruin everything I worked for. That's why when dude finally called me—dude who wanted to get at him—I ran right on out to the Devil's Cesspool off Farmers Boulevard. He was right where he said he'd be. All the way in the back, waiting at a table alone.

"What up?" he said.

"Chilling. Get right to it, homie. What this nigga did to you and what's in it for me?"

"I'm not going to get into what he did. All you need to concern yourself with is the money you gonna make."

"What you need me to do?"

"Just have him in a spot where I can get at him. You don't even have to be there."

"What makes you think I need money?"

"My man, you ain't shit. Yeah, your name out there, but your bitch and supplier are the brains behind the operation. You think niggas don't know that shit? Or is you really running around thinking you putting fear in somebody's heart? What the fuck was it you was doing before this? You was working for Carmello. That's your aim in life, nigga. You're a fucking worker."

"Yo, who the fuck do you think you talking to?"

I stood up and knocked his drink off the table.

"Chill out and stop making a scene. See, you not with your li'l bodyguards right now. So do yourself a favor and don't get hurt, son," he threatened, looking back towards five of his people playing pool.

"How much you talking, man?" I asked sitting back down.

"Ten g's. All you gotta do is get him to meet you. It'll be the easiest ten g's you ever made in your life. Sound like a good deal?"

"I'm wit' it. Word."

"I'll holla soon. One!" He got up and whirled his finger in the air alerting his men that it was time to bounce.

# CHAPTER FIFTY-FIVE

## *Carmello*

"It doesn't matter how well the streets know me, man. When Santiago went away, I was looked on as the snitch," I said to Manuel.

"Well, Mello. It is what it is. You are the one who left the confession on tape. So it is what you are, but you are not solely the reason why Miguel and Santiago serve time. Carlos is the component that bought their empire down. But it is a new day now. All is forgiven. Just do not ever turn on me, Mello, because I surely will murder you with no hesitation whatsoever. You see I don't like niggers at all, but for some reason you are the ones taking and selling all the drugs. Keeps me rich. Kept your parents rich. And the niggers can make you rich again."

This was it. I was going back into business. Fuck school. Fuck Cashmere. Shit was going to be different this time. I wasn't showing niggas no love. Shit. Nobody was showing me none.

Over the next couple of months I began putting together a deadly nest of snakes. I even recruited vixens to set the dudes up that were working under Cashmere.

This way, whenever it was time to pay Manuel, he'd come up short just when he thought he was at the height of his career. He'd have to come out of his own pocket to cover the losses. Competition would once more become reacquainted with me and never let Cashmere know I was orchestrating such jassy two-elevens. They didn't like it, but what the fuck was they gonna do?

Bitch-niggas' bodies were falling like the vertical rains of Katrina, as I stormed through the block, making X-Men out of these so-called made men. Some real muthafucking shit. Two months later, I was pushing a money green, two-door Continental Bentley. I was right back doing the shit I knew best. Ha. It's funny how you set out with the right intentions, but always come up fifty-cents short of an honest dollar. I know who I am and that ain't gonna change. All the fancy talk and vast vocabulary don't mean shit. I'm a killer and a drug-dealer to a politically incorrect society. Those social and economic FICA-driven slaves, look at me like I'm the one robbing them. But, to these zombies out here in the street, I'm like the president of the United States. That's what these crackers fear the most. The power and influence of a hustler. I'm no different from George Bush. He hustles war, dreams, lies, and oil. I juggle death and reality in biggies and bottles. Everybody gets high off something. If anybody's gonna kill my people, then why not let it be me, instead of these crackers that got us living in the box? I'm just keeping it in the family. I tried to trade these guns in and only came up with black roses. So now, use your vision and watch how I rock in this cold November rain.

# CHAPTER FIFTY-SIX

## *Santiago*

"The air smells so wonderful," Santiago stated, riding in the limousine. He was two days out of prison, and on his way to see Manuel. Previously, he'd stayed in a hotel hideaway down in Pennsylvania, waiting on his uncle to retrieve him to, once more, run the drug trade.

"I am happy to see you smile, nephew," Manuel said placing his hand on his lap.

"It is good to be free. I miss the business and look forward to joining you as partners. Has poppa asked of me yet?"

"He has no words for you."

"Uncle, you know that I was not to blame for this?"

"What has happened has happened. I do not spend time in the past."

"Have my wife and children been alerted of my release?"

"We're going to see them now."

"How is she? My wife."

"She looks just as she did when you left. They all look forward to your arrival."

"Very good, Uncle. What is your bother? Your responses seem to carry a little fiery weight to them."

"You lied to me."

"Never. What are you talking about?"

"I asked if you put the hit out on Carmello Junior. You told me you knew nothing of such."

"Uncle, there are some things that are personal. Carmello was of no consequence to you."

"But I asked and you denied." Santiago could almost sense where this was leading, but still took into consideration that they were family.

"So what do you insinuate, Uncle?"

"Your father, my brother, is in intensive care for the past six months."

"How is that? I would've received news of such incident."

"Not if it were made possible for you not to hear of such. He left news behind that you nor your family be entitled to anything upon your release. Your accounts have been cleaned out. He wants nothing to do with you."

"Why am I here with you then?"

"I have nothing to do with what my brother feels. You did not defy me, so I have no gripes with you. With me, it is business as usual. You are here to recreate everything that you and your foolish men destroyed. Everything my father and his father constructed."

"Si. You know I can do it. But I will no longer work with niggers. Especially the one I hear you have working for you named Cashmere."

"You won't have to. Trust me you won't have to."

"Poppa," Maria said hugging Santiago around the neck, as he and Manuel entered the tenth floor, Bronx apartment. Santiago couldn't believe his eyes. The furniture in the small two-bedroom apartment was third-hand. His children sat crowded around the twelve-inch snowy black and white television on the cushions of the two-legged couch. He gagged at the sight of cow-sized cockroaches running out of the garbage and under the refrigerator. Tears welled in his eyes, while he kissed his wife and hugged his children. Then anger boiled in the bottom of his stomach.

"What is this?" he asked walking through the slummy tenement apartment.

"I am sorry, poppa," Maria apologized. "I tried to straighten up before you got here. This was the best I could do."

He walked into the kitchen and opened the door to the refrigerator. The light inside flickered, as roaches ran around inside the bulb. He quickly closed it.

"Uncle. What is this? Why is my family living in this hell?"

"It is all welfare will provide."

"Welfare? What happened to my money?"

"It is vamoose. Did you think lawyers were free?"

"But we are familia."

"Si. That is why you are not dead. Be content with what you have."

"My wife and children cannot live in this filth. Why do you shame me like this?"

"Poppa, it is fine. Please do not argue your first day home. We've missed you."

"Listen to your wife, Santi." Santiago stared around once more, and sat on the cushion next to his children. He dropped his head into his hands and wept, feeling at an all-time low.

"Look at you. Do not further shame your family than you already have. Stand up and be a man." Maria dropped down beside him and she, along with the children, hugged him.

The pressure cooker's clicker in the kitchen began to rock back and forth, as steam shot out the pot's side.

"It smells as if comida is ready, Maria," Manuel said.

She kissed Santiago's forehead and ran into the kitchen. She used the oven mitts to place the pot under the cold running water.

"I shall return in exactly two hours, Santi. Be ready before I get back," Manuel said.

"You no stay to eat?" Maria asked.

"No, thank you. I do not dine with pigs," he laughed walking out the door.

# CHAPTER FIFTY-SEVEN

## Cashmere

"Something just doesn't add up. I hear Santiago's out of jail, and I still haven't gotten the word to do anything to Carmello."

"Why don't you forget about him and let's just leave. We have all the money we need. I fixed the books where Manuel will never know it's missing until we're long gone."

"It's just that easy, Lexi? Huh? I don't think so."

"Why not? I know him better than you do. I know places he dare not go."

"He'll kill us if he finds us."

"Why don't you get a back bone? I've been robbing Manuel for years now. I have lots of money, Cashmere. We can leave and never look back."

"What if he finds me?"

"Then why don't you kill him? Kill him and then you'll be in charge. Isn't that what you've always wanted in the first place? To be in charge. It's like, ever since Carmello came back into your life you've been slipping."

"Don't you worry about Carmello. I'm gonna take care of him."

"Yeah right. Since you been with Manuel, I've never seen you do nothing but pick up and deliver. Carmello on the other hand? His reputation speaks for itself. Maybe you're in the wrong business?" I slapped her in the face and she fell back into the coat rack.

"Stop trying to play me, before I have to show you a side you ain't used to, Lexi. You can think what you want, but I'll kill if I have to."

"You can't kill shit but the moment," she said wiping blood from the corner of her mouth.

"Keep thinking that. You go ahead and call up Manuel. If we gonna leave, then I gotta make sure he's dead first."

"Uh-uh. You have to be a man and do this on your own. I mean, don't you get it? All your workers are ending up dead because Carmello is working for Manuel."

"Why would he hire Carmello to kill his own men?"

"Damn. This shit really isn't for you. Think about it, Cash. Carmello robs the workers, then you pay for it out of your pocket and Carmello redistributes it right back out there. You the only one in the dark." The more she spoke, the more heated I got. His bitch-ass was dead.

"How you know so much?" I asked her.

"I've worked with criminals my entire life, hon. See, this here, is something you pursued. I was born into this life. It pacifies me. Without it, I don't know where I'd be. White collar crime. It's just as dangerous as any other illegal business, but the rush is just so exhilarating when you know the feds are a second off your butt. Then they lose that paper trail and have to start all over again."

"I gotta make a call." I said.

"Do what you do, just do it right. There is no time for mistakes."

She turned me on so much when she talked like that. I

grabbed her by the hand and pulled her to the couch. I pushed her onto it and slid my hand up her skirt. No panties as usual. She cracked her legs further apart and guided my hand up and down her wet pussy. She stuck her hand down there and played with herself. She then lay across the couch and pulled her skirt off. Hard as hell, I inserted myself with no hesitation. With one of her legs hanging off the couch, and the other on my shoulder, I maneuvered in and out frantically. It felt so warm and homey, like the shit was made just for me. She grabbed the back of my head with one hand and pulled me down to kiss her. Our tongues wrestled until they became bow-tied. It was far from being considered love-making, but like I had said earlier, she was a good fuck. Five minutes later, it was over just as quickly as it started.

After showering, she got dressed and bounced. I waited for her to pull out of the driveway before I started rambling through the bedroom for anything that could tell me more of who she was. Pussy will make you sleep and I should've been more on my A-game a long time ago. She had nothing I could find to prove that she was living foul. Still, I had a feeling something was really wrong and it wasn't just about Mello and Manuel.

# CHAPTER FIFTY-EIGHT

## *Carmello*

"Hey, Tarsha," I said through my cell in the parking lot of Burger King in Elmont.

"Hi, baby. I miss you," she said. "Are you alright out there?"

"I'm fine. You okay out there?"

"I'm good. I went to the doctor today."

"Yeah? What's the matter?"

"I'm two months pregnant."

"Word? That's good. Don't worry about anything. I'll be home soon."

"I hope so, because I don't want to do this alone."

"You won't have to. I promise when this money gets right, I'll be back. We're going to make it baby."

"You sound so much better than you did before I left. I must've been stressing you out?"

"Naw. I just didn't want anything to happen to you."

"I've been watching the news, baby. Things are looking as if they're getting worse and worse out there everyday. I hope you're not involved in any of that?"

"Baby, I'm doing whatever it takes to get to the bottom of this bullshit."

"And what's that?"

"Tarsha, I'm going to holla at you soon, okay, baby? Please don't be worried. I'm out here doing big things for us."

"Please don't get yourself in trouble. You know I'm not about the money. Just get back here safely."

"Will do. I'm out." Tarsha was really in my corner. She's the kind of woman that made a man want to give her the world. I couldn't go back to her broke, expecting her to take care of a grown-ass man while she worked. What woman would ever respect a healthy dude, who's not bringing in some paper?

My father did it for my mother. He did whatever it was he had to do to keep her happy. It's just too bad it got them both killed. I wasn't going to let that happen to me or my woman. Santiago destroyed my life. The feds took all my money. I was surviving off instincts and desire. What society doesn't understand, is that sometimes we have to do grimy thangs to survive. I mean, I had the opportunity to get into school and shit, but your destiny is your destiny. Look at my options. What else do you really think I could've accomplished at this time in my life? This is how hundreds of brothers feel everyday. Who the fuck really wanted to work some bullshit job starting at the bottom, watching white kids with less credentials than a nigga, still come out on top. And all we receive for our efforts is sweetbread and pork chops, sitting next to some house-nigga named Rodney Coon, slapping his knee and playing the banjo, waiting on a nickel raise every six months. Yeah. You know what I'm talking about. See, the government has woven the most intricate and sticky pattern of deception to entrap us in a transparent web of genocidal, premeditative, entanglement and illusion. You'd better believe it.

A knock on the window at my side of the car snapped me out of my 'each one, teach one' soliloquy. I instinctively put my hand around the trigger of my glock, before looking up. A dorky-looking white boy stood there sipping a cup of steaming coffee.

"What's up, son?" I asked.

"Carmello, right?" Wasn't no mistaking that this dick was five-o.

"What can I do for you, officer?" He looked as if he was in shock that his cover was blown so quickly.

"Ha. I guess I'm losing it. Can we talk?"

"I ain't got nothing to say to you, man. What you got to talk to me about?"

"You've been off the scene for quite awhile, but now, it looks like things are looking bright again," he said tapping the hood of my car.

"I don't know what you talking about, yo."

"Turn off the car and let me talk to you for a minute."

"Fuck you."

"Look man. I know about Tarsha and the pregnancy. Don't you want to be there for her when your child is born?"

There was no need to even contemplate how he got that information. The government had access to everything and anything a nigga was involved with.

"What she got to do with this?"

"Nothing yet. If you want to keep it that way, turn off the car, man. I just want to talk to you."

"Shit! Shit! Shit!" I yelled banging both hands on the steering wheel. "Alright. We can talk, but not here."

"Okay. I'm going to be straight with you, Carmello. You're being watched by everybody. Your every move, since you've landed, has been recorded by surveillance video."

"So. I ain't been doing nothing," I said as we walked through One-seventy-six Park in Laurelton, Queens."

"Carmello, I thought you quit this business. I thought you were finished with it and trying to get your life together in California."

"Look, if you feel you got something on me, then arrest me now."

"We don't want you if we can help it."

"How I know you are who you say you are? What's your name?"

"Detective Shudemall," he answered, showing his badge and identification.

"So. I can get one of them shits made by the Koreans on Jamaica Avenue."

"Can they make one of these too?" he asked, pulling out a large manila envelope from the inside of his jacket. "Here. Take it. Look at the contents inside."

"What's inside? Some kind of set up or something."

"Not hardly. Go ahead and take a look." I pulled out four large pictures from the yellow envelope and he shined his flashlight on them. By the time I got to the fourth one, they dropped from my hands and I stood motionless. He immediately scooped them up and slipped them back inside the envelope.

"You convinced yet?" he asked.

"How'd you get those?" I asked still stunned.

He'd shown me two photos of China in the parking lot of the Holiday Inn. A photo of me and Manuel picking up and making deliveries on the block, and a photo of me shooting up that block on 232$^{nd}$ and Linden Boulevard.

"There is nothing that goes on anywhere that we do

not know about. Especially when it comes to Blacks and Spanish people. Sorry to come off as a racist, but you know the routine. We've been watching your family since you were a kid. At headquarters, we even have photos of when your parents took you, your brother, and sister to Great Adventures. You remember that day? The day when China was too short to ride the roller coaster, so you stayed on the ground with her while the rest of your family rode it."

"Alright, man. What the fuck do you want with me?"

"Not you, Santiago. He was just recently released from prison. I'm sure from being around Manuel you already know that. We think that Manuel is going to kill him. Do you know anything about that?"

"Naw."

"Come on, man. Your freedom is on the line here. It'll only take a second for my back-up to get here and have you bought up on charges of distribution, murder, and conspiracy to commit murder."

"That's bullshit and you know it. The shit would never hold up in court. Those two photos of me are blurry as shit, so I ain't never scared. You don't have guns. You don't have drugs. And ain't nobody going to tell you shit."

"Damn, man. You used to be so much smarter than this. Now I can see how easy it was for Santiago to put a hit out on you. By the way? How's your health? I see you're not walking with the sticks any more."

"Fuck you!"

"Carmello, why did you come back? You were back in school, pretty girlfriend, kid on the way. What are you doing, man?"

"Whatever I got to do to survive."

"Manuel is Santiago to the fifth power. He'll destroy everything you have. Anything you can think of, he will take from you."

"Like the feds did?"

"You wanna look at it like that? Then yeah. Just like
the feds did. The thing I don't understand about guys
like you, is that you got the potential, intelligence, and
drive to run a corporate company. But yet you'd rather
fuck around out here until somebody pops you in the
head, or you go to jail for life."

"Look. Don't give me that bullshit. It's because of guys
like you that my family is dead."

"Wrong! Your father is the reason why your family is
dead. If it wasn't for him, you wouldn't be doing this
now. I'm not going to waste much more time trying to
pull you out this rut, Carmello. The choice is yours. I can
help you if you want to help yourself. Think about it.
Here's my card. I'm telling you now that you don't have
a lot of time."

As he walked away, a car pulled up to the entrance of
the park and he got in. He looked at me before it drove
off and pointed down to his watch.

Weeks had passed and I heard nothing from the detective. I started watching my back just a little bit more and
sent Tarsha money twice a week to put away for us.
Everything was looking lovely and it was almost beginning to feel like old times, minus Caine and China. At
least I didn't have to continuously monitor their actions
anymore. I remember there being a time when I regretted
being in this game. But now I see why my father did it for
so long. I'd never have to stand on the back of no line at
the check cashing place, fuming over why they needed to
take out a percentage for cashing it. The bank was the
same way. Now I was making so much money, I didn't
even know how much I had in my dummy account.
There's an old saying, "If you know exactly how much
gwop you got in the bank, then you don't got enough in
the bank."

I deposited a healthy amount of money into the bank and the rest into the safe that I had purchased from Combinations 'R' Us. I closed the pantry-styled door of my closet in the bathroom of the condo Manuel bought for me, then fell to the couch. There was a knock at my door and I grabbed my gun off the coffee table. I lived in a gated community, so the only person that knew I was here was Manuel. It had to be that fucking detective. These niggas was off the chain and could find pebbles in Bedrock with the technology they had. Shit!

Bam! Bam! Bam!

The loud knocking on the door rattled the mirrors on my wall. I cautiously walked to it and looked through the peephole on a right angle.

"What the fuck?" I said opening it and pointing the gun at Lexi. "What in the hell are you doing here and how'd you find me?" I asked cocking the gun. "Better start talking real fast, or you about to be a real dead bitch."

"I had nowhere else to go. Cashmere is at home acting crazy. He's been snorting the product."

"Don't play with me," I said pushing her head with the muzzle. I looked up and down the hallway, before closing the door. "Get over there."

She moved into the livingroom and stood motionless in the middle of the floor.

"Throw me your purse," I demanded. She tossed it over to me and I dumped out all its contents. There was nothing but her wallet and some lip-gloss, which could have easily been concealing some microphone-type shit, so I stomped it.

"You know how much that cost?" she coolly asked.

"Yeah. A lot less than your funeral. Talk!"

"I already told you. Cashmere is over there bugging out. He's snorting the shit and cutting the product in the streets with rat poison."

"What the fuck that gotta do with me? You know what? Strip bitch! You wearing a wire or something?"

"Strip?" she repeated, looking at me like I was speaking some foreign language.

"You need me to say it in languages you understand? Jouhen. Desmontar. Desosser."

"Imbecile," she said in French.

"Chienne," I retaliated.

"Pendejo," she said rolling her eyes.

"Alright. Enough of this shit," I said slapping her face. She started coming out of her clothes, until she was standing stark-naked in my livingroom.

"Now talk."

"I came here to warn you."

"Warn me of what?"

"Cashmere wants to kill you."

"You his girl. Why you warning me?"

"I can't tell you that. Just trust me when I say that it is information beneficial to both of us."

"How'd you find out where I lived?"

"I can't tell you that either. But if you kill me now, you'll never know what else is going on." I stared at her long and hard in absolute silence, before moving closer to her.

"What's going on? All y'all muthafuckas in this together? All the sudden everybody wants to warn Carmello."

"Who's everybody?"

"The shit doesn't matter. Just get dressed."

"You're going to kill me. Aren't you?"

"Naw. I ain't never killed no woman before." Looking at her standing there in the nude with her titties jumping out at me made me forget all about Tarsha. With this gun, I could do whatever I wanted, but I didn't get down like that. I knew she did.

"Why do you keep staring at me like that?" she asked.

"You got a nice body for a straight criminal."

"You really like what you see?" she said, massaging her breasts and walking closer towards me.

"That's far enough," I said raising my gun at her again.

"Relax, babe, Lexi's not going to hurt you," she insisted still moving closer. It had been a couple of months since I felt the touch of a woman. I was trying my best to stay true to Tarsha, especially since she was having my baby. I hated to use that sorry-ass excuse of being a man, to pick a time like this to become weak. She kissed me and put her hand over the hand that was holding the gun. I raised it above my head and pushed her down by the shoulder, onto her knees. She unzipped my pants and my dick jumped out like a spring, and bounced. Looking up into my eyes, she placed her warm lips around it and applied immediate and maximum pleasure to my zone. Twisting and turning her head she let it slide in and out the corners of both sides of her mouth. Spitting on the tip of it, she slopped it back up in one long, drawn-out suction, that made me buckle at the knees. I dropped to the floor and lay across the black carpet.

She unbuckled my pants, while I kicked out of them. Impatiently awaiting for her to reapply her mojo, she got back to work stabbing the tip of her tongue deep inside my navel, then circled its structure. Her cheeks sucked in with every stroke she took, and the thick veins in my dick pulsated.

"Fuck me," she said turning on her back. "Come on, baby. You know you want to." She was right. I did want to. I wasn't worried about violating Cashmere. He wasn't my man no more. So we did it. And we did the damn thing well. But at the same time, I really wasn't into it. I wanted to be with Tarsha. I was missing her so bad and I put all of my hurt, heart, and pain into Lexi. For a moment, it almost felt like I was making love—love to my life. Love to the game. Love to everything I lost. With each pump inside of her, I felt a piece of me fade away, and when the nut was released, I felt my soul follow behind it. I pulled out of her with tears running down my face.

"Don't stop, baby," she said pulling me back down.

"Get off me," I said snatching myself away.

"What?"

"Get out!" I said getting dressed. There was another knock at the door. I grabbed my gun again and looked down at Lexi. She started throwing her clothes on. I opened the door without even questioning who it was. There stood Manuel with my gun pointed directly between his eyes.

"Is that a gun in your hand, or are you just happy to see me?" he asked.

"Now it's a party," I said looking back at Lexi.

"Oh. And what a party it is," he smiled looking at me and her.

"So you told her how to find me?"

"But of course. Who else? I thought you might be lonely and find comfort in such a pretty woman, such as the one back in California. Was the comparison to your liking?" he asked kissing Lexi's lips.

"Hardly," I responded.

"You were not satisfied with the quality of my gift to you?"

"I think he was," Lexi said.

"I hear that you were having conversations with Detective Shudemall," Manuel said, removing his hat, taking a seat on the couch. "I hope you haven't been being a tattle-tale?"

"I didn't tell him anything."

"Very good. There is much to be done and we do not need interference from the pigs."

"Work like what? We don't pick up until tomorrow."

"There is someone I'd like you to become reacquainted with."

"I'm gonna have to meet with you later. I got something to take care of."

"That is fine. But let me tell you something."

"What?"

"Don't you fuck me. I've been very good to you. Call me when you are finished your business. Come, Lexi. We must be going."

"I really enjoyed myself," she said to me smiling, then kissed my cheek.

# CHAPTER FIFTY-NINE

## *Cashmere*

"So just give up what you know, man. We have all the evidence we need to put you away for life already," Detective Shudemall said to me.

Can you believe that earlier, I got pulled over for a fucking traffic violation? This guy had been on my ass for the past couple of years, just waiting for me to fuck up. And now he had me on a bullshit, blown-out tail-light charge. I guess what really did it was the $500 I offered him to rip up the ticket and let me go. See these fuckers was always tight with me, because they could never catch me with anything. But association is a muthafucka.

"I'm only going to ask you this once, Cashmere. Where are you getting the shit from? Better yet, where is Manuel getting it from?"

"Here you go. Man, how long we gonna do this for?"

"Give me a minute alone with this guy," he said to the officer inside the interrogation room with us. "Alright. Cut the fucking tough-guy act and give me something. You're the one that called me and said Carmello was back in town."

"I called you because you said if he ever came back into town to call you."

"And why do you think I told you to do that?"

"I don't know, man. You miss him? Shit. Why you sweating me?"

Shudemall looked out the window of the wooden door and turned down the blinds.

"What you doing, man?" I asked.

"Too much light coming through there. You don't mind, right?"

"Shit. It's your office."

"You're absolutely right. It is my office. My house. My rules. Those are all my brothers out there and we all stick together. Get my drift? Now, I'm going to ask you a different question? Where is Manuel getting his shit from?"

"I want a lawyer."

"You're not getting a fucking lawyer!" he yelled, slamming my head on the table. "I've been real nice to you up until now."

"Man why don't you chill? This is police brutality."

"You wanna see some police brutality you stupid nigger. I'll show you police brutality." He walked out the office and returned with three more suits.

"What's this? I thought it was just me and you."

"You wanted to see police brutality? I'm gonna give you your wish."

"Chill out, man. Just chill. I'll tell you what you want to know."

"Okay fellas. I'll call you back in if I need ya."

"Why you fucking with me? I pay you every month."

"It's not working anymore. The CIA is doing some serious crackdowns. I need names and places now."

"Damn," I said, with my face in my hands.

"You wanted to be a hustler, but you can't hustle. We're the real hustlers. We let you and the rest of the niggers do all the foot work for us, then we collect. It's always been that way. After all this time, I can't understand for the life of me, why none of you's have never caught on. See, the city is like one big slave ship and we have all you niggers bunched up and piled on top of one another, pissing and shitting on each other because there's nowhere else to go. Dumb asses. Then here's the real kicker. While we got you's all bunched up on this ship, we even managed to get you buying your own chains to keep you locked down. Sure they're not as heavy as the originals, but it still does the job. It's like you's all fighting to keep staying slaves. Robbing each other for chains and shit. Then you wonder why our kids get the better education. Wanna know why?"

"Not really."

"It's because it's in their blood to run a tight ship," he laughed. "Get it? Tight ship! And it's in your peoples blood to always drop the anchor and stay stagnated in the middle of the ocean. Ya smell me?" he asked folding his arms in a b-boy stance. "Alright. History lesson one is over. Talk to me."

I thought that was it for me, but he let me go. I had to do what I had to do. I couldn't do no time in prison. I had to get my cake together and bounce. I should've listened to Lexi when I had the chance. We should've just bounced. I can't believe Manuel had Mello working for him. Now everything was beginning to make sense. No matter if I told or not, Manuel was planning to kill me. He wanted Mello to take my place, which meant that he'd probably get him to kill me. I think it was time I called up Enoch to take care of this. With Mello gone, I could handle Manuel through Lexi.

"Enoch. What up, playa?"

"Cash. I'ma make that happen tonight. Where you wanna do this at, son?"

# CHAPTER SIXTY

## *Carmello*

Me and Lexi drove out to Manuel's home in White-stone. He said he had a surprise for me. I was sure it was some more product he wanted me to take back into Queens, so one of his guys could get it packed up to be flown out to Texas. What I liked about Manuel, was he paid me anytime I had to go through the toll to cross the bridge. We had some real sweet shit going on. Lexi had been quiet the whole ride.

"What's with you?" I asked.

"I have to act in front of Manuel. But I didn't appreciate you putting that gun on me."

"Are you fucking kidding me? You put a gun to my head in Cashmere's house. You lucky I didn't shoot you."

"Can't you drive any faster?"

"No. I don't need to be pulled over. I hate having to explain myself to cops. What's your rush? We both going to the same place."

"Hurry up past that toll. I need a fix."

"Oh no. You sniff that shit?"

"Don't you dare get ready to judge me. Just drive the car, babe."

She rolled up her window and pulled out the small bag with the soda in it. First she dipped her pinky finger in it, and spread it across her gums. Then she poured the rest on a piece of folded paper and tilted in her nose. She took a huge sniff and seconds later sneezed twice.

"Oh God," she said rolling the window back down. "Manuel has the purest form of soda. It's never cut."

"That's real good to know," I responded in disgust. I'm glad we were almost there. I couldn't stand being around no fucking junkies. I knew there was something funny about her. I should've peeped that out about her with all that sniffling. Twenty minutes later, we were at his house. Manuel was out on his front lawn talking to a neighbor.

"Mello. Lexi." He welcomed us with open arms as we strolled up the walkway.

He kissed me on both sides of my cheeks and, of course, kissed Lexi's lips. There was no doubt in my mind that this nigga was high as hell.

"What's up, Manny?" I said. "Are we going to go inside?"

"Sure. Sure. Hey, didn't I promise you a surprise?"

"What you got for me, poppi?" Lexi asked

"For you, my little mommi, I have the finest." We walked up a spiral staircase into a bedroom, with two bathrooms inside. To the left was a balcony facing the backyard, with a trail that led deep into the woods. On the glass lunch table sat a bottle of scotch and a small wooden box.

"Sit," he said pulling out a chair for Lexi.

"So what's the surprise, man? Cops in the closet?"

"Time. First we drink," he said filling our glasses.

"You don't think it's kinda cold out here, man?" I asked.

"What you talk? This is my kind of weather. Lexi, isn't this your kind of weather?"

"Si, poppi," she responded, opening the lid of the small wooden box.

"Mello. Do you want I turn up the heat?" he asked.

"Naw, man. I'm good."

"I have outdoor heating."

"Manuel, I said I'm good."

Lexi set up a pile of white on a coaster beside the box. Picking up a straw, she began sniffing with her left thumb over her right nostril.

"Oh, I feel so good. This is the best," Lexi said tilting her head back.

"Have a drink," Manuel said filling my glass half-way.

Manuel reached for the small wooden box and sniffed his fair share of that get-high.

"Aaah," he exhaled with a smile on his face. He pushed the box over towards me. "Try."

"I don't do that shit man."

"Come, Mello. It'll take Diablo off your back," he added, taking his drink down in one large gulp. The doorbell rang from the back of the house.

"You expecting company?" I asked staring at the box.

"We're expecting company."

"We?"

"I will be right back. Lexi, why don't you show Mello how to have a good time. Give me five minutes."

"It wasn't loaded," Lexi said out of nowhere.

"What wasn't loaded?"

"The day at Cashmere's house. It wasn't loaded. I would've never really shot you, but I had to get you off of Manuel's investment," she confessed, pulling the box back to her.

"I'm supposed to believe that? I don't believe shit anymore."

"That is up to you."

"Why are you telling me this?"

She looked around and listened out for Manuel's foot-steps to start back up the stairs.

"I've been working for Manuel for a long time. He has millions of dollars in an account only I know of. He doesn't know I know about it."

"And?"

"He is feeding you peanuts. You nor Cashmere are the first he has used to move his product. There is no way he will let you walk away from this alive. When he has all that he needs, he will kill you."

"You're telling me this because?"

"I have a plan."

"I'm listening."

"With all the connects you've gained since working by his side, you can take his place if he was to mysteriously turn up dead."

"How do you think that would work? Who do you think the feds or his people would go looking for first?"

"Cashmere. While everybody is on his trail, we could empty out Manuel's accounts and never look back. You could go your way, and I'd go mine. There'd never be a need to come back to New York again."

"Why are you coming to me with this?"

"Because, as of right now, you are the only one close enough to touch him. For some reason he seems to like you. Not even Cashmere has been to this home. It says a lot."

"Okay. Let's just say you're on the up and up, why am I here today? What is the big surprise?"

"That is why it is called a surprise, Carmello. I promise you will love it though."

"Carmello. Come down. It is time for the surprise."

"Why don't you try some of this to calm your nerves?"

"No," I said pushing it away. "I'm going down."

When I got downstairs, Manuel was waiting by the front door with it wide open.

"It is time for us to leave. Our chariot awaits."

There was a chauffer standing by the door of a black limousine in the driveway.

"You bought me a limo?" I asked.

"It is what will take us to your surprise." At that point I began to get a little bit nervous. I really began to think about what Lexi had said. I wondered if this would be my final ride. I shrugged it off though, and opted to take the ride anyway.

"Manny. May I come?" Lexi asked, running down the steps as he was pulling the front door after him.

"You stay. I am expecting important calls you must attend to. I will be home later. Do not put too much up your nose."

# CHAPTER SIXTY-ONE

## *Carmello*

"Now I want you to stay right here until I call for you," Manuel said after the limo pulled across the street from a project building in the BX. As people walked by the tinted-windows, pedestrians strained their eyes to see through them. It was nowhere near prom night for high schoolers, so more than likely they assumed it might be a superstar. But when Manuel exited, they lost interest. He held up one finger at me before running across the street and hopping over the divider towards the building.

"Hello?" I answered my phone.

"Mello, what up nigga? I hear you back, son," said Cashmere.

"I been hearing a lot of shit about you, Cash."

"Oh yeah? I might say the same about you partna. You been doing some real foul shit. I know about everything."

"What you know about, nigga?"

"You running with Manuel? You cock-blocking, bitch-ass nigga."

"I'm not running with anybody. And even if I was, what the fuck you going to do about it?"

"You'll see."

"You know what, man, do what you gots to do. You know I will."

"So fuck it then, nigga. Let's just handle this. Where you wanna do this at?"

"I'll see you," I concluded, disconnecting the call. My phone chirped as soon as the call was disconnected. Manuel was alerting me with a message that simply read, "Ten E." I took a deep breath and took my gun off safety. I didn't trust elevators, so I walked up the stairs. The extra time would give me a while to think on what this was all about. As I closed in on the tenth floor, the smell of piss and spilled beer began to increase. The dim lights flashed on and off. The paint on the metal banisters was rusting, and the walls were covered with graffiti. I crept up on the green door leading to the hallway and peeped through the meshed glass window. There was no doorknob, so I had to slowly pull the door open by sticking my two fingers in the hole. It had been so long since I'd been in the projects, I almost forgot what its hallways could smell like. Powerful odors of Caribbean and Spanish-scented aromas clashing with one another. Careless people smoking cigarettes, crack, and weed. The horrible stench of garbage hanging out the disposal chute. I was almost ready to throw up. I stood at the end of the hallway until I saw the light from apartment Ten E spread across the floor. Manuel's head popped out and he quietly flagged me down.

"Hurry, hurry," he whispered. As I walked down towards him, I pulled out my gun just in case it was some kind of set up. When I walked in, I didn't know whether to flip out or just break down and shoot everybody. Sitting on the couch was a badly beaten Santiago. I guess we were both surprised at one another's presence, because when he saw me, I could swear he straight shitted his pants.

"Surprise!" Manuel said smiling, while patting my back. "Here is the man that killed your family."

Before Santiago could say a word, I walked right up to him and put two in his head.

"And that's that!" Manuel said spitting on his corpse. "You turn on your family, you die." Enraged, I began punching and kicking his body.

"You stupid muthafucka. I hate your ass. Kill my sister? My family?" The men who had beat him down, ran out of the apartment while I continued taking out my aggression on a dead man.

"Carmello, let us go. Now."

I damn-near jumped down those ten flights of stairs and ran out the lobby, straight to the limo. Manuel followed soon after. The chauffeur took off and we were on our way to visit Cashmere next.

"How do you feel, Mello?" Manuel asked, positioning his sunglasses.

"Like shit. What I just did won't bring anybody back. Why'd you bring me here to do that?"

"Revenge is sweet. He betrayed my brother, his father. You deserve not to live after such. Isn't it what you always wanted? To get back at him."

"I guess so, man."

"Never guess. Be sure! It is what you wanted to do. Si?"

"Yeah. I wish I could rewind time and do it again."

"I feared also that he may have still been conversing with the pigs. Telling them of my present operations to be released early. He brought his condition onto himself. He betrayed everything my family has worked long and hard for."

"So why didn't you do it yourself?"

"I would be connected too easily."

"What about his family? His wife. Won't she suspect?"

"It is already taken care of. It is a shame how one apple can spoil the whole bunch. She and Santi will be together soon."

"Your own family, man? How can you stand it?"

"It is the nature of the game. It no matter who you are. You violate the codes, you will suffer or perish. No matter gender or age. You cannot continue watching your back for the rest of your life, wondering if an enemy's child will grow up looking for a little revenge. All you have in this world is family, and once they turn on you, who can you trust?"

Manuel pulled out his nose medicine and alleviated his stress. He handed me some and this time I experimented. He handed me the short straw and I inhaled it through my nostril and my body began to tingle instantly. A bitterness formed in the back of my throat and it felt as if I didn't have a care in the world. I felt like I was experiencing an eternal nut. It was a sensation impeccably unexplainable.

"Let it take you away, Mello. It will ease your mind. You feel good, no?"

"My heart is beating fast as hell."

"That means it is working. Have some more." I indulged in two more lines and felt as if nothing else existed except me and the white pony. I rode it off into the sunset until my eyes closed for the duration of the trip.

# CHAPTER SIXTY-TWO

## *Cashmere*

"Where the fuck you been, Lexi?" I yelled at her as she entered through the front door, high as hell.

"I'm feeling real good right now. Don't mess up my high."

"Where you been the past three days, huh? You been out fucking, Manuel?"

"That's what you want to hear? Then yes. I been out fucking, Manuel. I fucked Carmello, too. How you like that?" she said, fixing her hair in the full-length mirror on the wall.

"You been with Mello?"

"And it was good too." I punched her in back of the head and she dropped to the floor.

"I'm sick and tired of niggas try'na play me. I'm making doe and still I ain't getting no respect. Fuck that. Get up, bitch. You wanna talk gangsta, then I'ma knock you out like you gangsta."

"Hit me all you want to. You a pussy. I ain't never seen you do that to no man. You wouldn't dare, because you too scared."

"You think so?"

"I know so," she said. I pulled her to her feet and pushed her head into the mirror.

"You been real disrespectful, since that nigga Mello came into town. I don't care if you is Manuel's girl. I'll pop your ass right now."

"Go ahead. I dare you. Matter of fact? I want you to."

"Don't fuck with me, Lexi."

"I ain't begun to fuck with you yet. I thought we was going to take care of Manuel. Are you scared to do it?"

"I ain't scared of shit. I just need to handle Mello first."

"What sense does it make to kill him? He's not the one with the money, the connects. Use your head and chase the man with the paper, Cashmere."

"I'm on it. Still, Mello's ass is gone tonight. I got somebody for his ass. I'm going to the bathroom to take a shit." While I sat on the bowl dumping out last night's dinner, I thought about how smart I really was. Detective Shudemall wanted all this information. I could give it to him now.

First, I'd get Lexi to get to Manny's doe. Then, get her on tape saying this shit about killing him. Then I'd pop his ass when he came to collect his doe for the week. Who'd get the blame when he got that confession?

Enoch was gonna kill Mello, but before that, he was gonna get his doe. We'd both take him to his rest and get him to empty out the safe. I'd have a nigga on standby outside, so soon as me and Enoch walked out, his ass would get sprayed. My mind could work real ill at times, and this plan was sick. Word up! Now who's gangsta, Carmello?

# CHAPTER SIXTY-THREE

## *Carmello*

Inever thought I'd be getting high off my own supply. But here I was, up for the second night in a row sniffing like there was no tomorrow. I guess it was bound to happen sooner or later. When you're selling this shit as a career, you eventually try it out. Whether it be that hard or soft, you will succumb to your master. And when I say your master, I mean to say that drugs don't work for us. We work for the drugs.

I don't know what was going through my mind that day I took Manuel up on his offer to sniff this shit. Maybe deep down inside, I was always just a little curious. But never in three lifetimes did I ever think I'd voluntarily induct myself into the very nostrils of the white house. Any which way, it was finally time to pay Cashmere a visit. But it wasn't going to be on his terms. Maybe I could save his life again before I'd have to kill his ass, or before he tried to kill me instead. A connect of mines told me where he'd be kicking it on a Friday night. Turns out I wasn't the only one experimenting. There was a tittie spot out in Corona, Queens named Jonesy's. I took a couple of cats out there with me, because I knew this fool hardly ever rolled alone.

It seemed that Manuel's name was no longer a threat to niggas, knowing that his top dog was a fucking crackhead. I walked through the front door and ordered myself a quick shot of vodka from the bar. The security guard near the DJ booth gave me a head nod towards the back exit. I passed him a hundred-dollar bill and walked straight out there.

"Cash," I said. He was getting his dick sucked while sucking on that glass dick. It dropped from his hands and broke. The dick-sucking trick looked up at him.

"How the fuck you gonna drop the shit, homie?" the homosexual, bitch-made, Brokeback mountaineer said.

"Yeah, nigga. Caught with your pants down," I said to Cashmere. "Get the fuck out of here." The fag, crack-head wiped his mouth and ran down the dark alley. Cashmere couldn't say shit. He was caught out there fucking with a homo and smoking the rock.

"Pull your fucking pants up, nigga. Your ass is exposed. Fucking homo-ass nigga. I always knew you was a little bitch." He quietly pulled up his pants and leaned against the brick wall.

"It ain't what it looked like," he aimlessly explained.

"Then what is it like, nigga? You out here getting blown by a crack-head and smoking the shit too. But that's you. I'm hearing a lot of shit, Cash. You calling me up talking shit too. So here I am. What it do, son?"

"You know what it do. You played me dude."

"That's not the way I hear it. You fucking with the police? You told that detective when I landed. For what?"

"I wasn't about to let you come back home and take away my shine. I was your bitch for years, while you talked to me like a son—son. Nobody cared who I was. Now I'm somebody that niggas know and respect."

"You really think that?" I laughed. "You talking to a nigga that grew up in this. A nigga that's a second-generation dealer. My father thought he was respected too. I ain't even going to front. I thought I had that love too, but at the end of the day, it's all about fear. For you to survive in this shit, niggas got to fear you. Cashmere? Ain't nobody afraid of you."

"There you go patronizing me again."

"You stupid muthafucka. I'm trying to save your life again. You see what happened to me right?" I said pulling up my shirt. "Look at these bullet scars, nigga. This look like respect to you? This is the real part of the game."

"So what. I got shot before too. Then what you do? Ax a nigga."

"The only reason you still here is because I axed you. Why can't you understand that?"

"You ain't never cared about nobody but yourself. That's why you did me dirty with Manny."

"I did you dirty? Manny did you dirty. You so fucking stupid, you can't even comprehend why he put me in your place. You ain't making as much doe no more. Know why? Because I got your money, playa. You'll always be a substitute, nigga."

"Think so?"

"I know so."

"I got your substitute. Your time is coming."

"Fuck all this talk. Something you wanna do to me? Here I am. Don't pass no messages through no bitch. Lexi ain't on your team. She a fucking coke-head bitch," I said pulling out my gun.

"So, what now? You gonna murder me out here after everybody seen you walk out here? You that bold?"

"Naw. I'm not going to kill you. You not a threat to no-body but yourself. Your career is over, nigga. Get your

homo ass up outta here, before I change my mind."
Cashmere went to walk inside, but I stopped him.

"Naw, nigga. Go that way," I said, pointing him out the alley.

"Next time I hear my name come out your mouth, I *will* kill you. Don't make me have to."

He walked down the short alley, occasionally looking back, not sure if I'd shoot or not.

# CHAPTER SIXTY-FOUR

## *Cashmere*

Not knowing who to turn to about Mello threatening my life, I called on Manny. He met me at the rest, with Lexi riding shot gun in the passenger seat.

"What is the emergency?" he asked.

"I got some disturbing news about your new number-one guy."

"What's that?"

"I was at the strip joint in Corona and walked out back to smoke a cig, and caught this nigga smoking that rock."

"Is that what you called me all the way over here for?"

"He was getting his dick sucked by a dude."

"I do not believe you. You are beginning to become a nuisance, Cashmere."

"What? This nigga can tell you anything and you believe him. He smoking your shit and fucking niggas, and you tell me I'm lying?"

"I want you out of my house by tomorrow. You are no longer of any benefit to me. I know a crack-head when I see one and you, mi amigo, fit the description to a tee."

"Oh. It's like that? After all the money I made for you?

Then you got that nigga shooting your own workers to get more money from me?"

"When I return mañana, I do not want to see you here."

"It's like that? Okay, come on, Lexi. Let's go."

"I'm not going anywhere with you."

"You turning on me too?"

"I never was on your side. When will you understand what this is really all about? It's about money. No more. No less." She winked her eye at me, as Manuel pulled out the driveway. Soon after, my cell phone rang.

"Hello?"

"Cashmere. This is Detective Shudemall. You make any decisions yet?"

"I sure have."

If niggas was gonna shit on me, then I was gonna take everybody down.

"You want me to meet you?" he asked.

"I name the place. It's getting to where I can't trust nobody."

"Didn't I tell you that? You're a good kid, Cashmere. This game ain't for you."

"That's what I keep hearing. One." The instant I hung up, the phone rang again.

"My nigga. What happened to you the other night? Where son at?" Enoch asked.

"You got the paper?"

"Been had that, dukes. Stop faking moves. You gonna bring this nigga or what?"

"I got you, mayne. Just need a lil' more time. The dude mad suspicious of everything."

"I'm getting suspicious of you."

"It ain't even like that."

"I hope not." The line disconnected. I went into the house to strap up, then hit the road.

I met up with Shudemall on a rooftop in Brooklyn. He was looking over the ledge at the lights on top of the Empire State Building.

"Detective." He quickly turned around.

"You packing?" he asked.

"You know that."

"Toss me the clip." I did so and he placed it on the roof's ledge.

"What you got for me?"

"Anything you want."

"Why the change of heart all of a sudden?"

"I thought you wanted the info?"

"Alright. Start snitching, I mean talking," he said sparking a cigarette.

I told him even more than I said before. I mean everything. Everybody was definitely going down.

"So when this all goes down, what happens to me?"

"If everything you say is true, and we can get some convictions going, then we'll place you in the witness protection program. You'll never be able to come back to New York again."

"Do I get some money for this?"

"I believe that can be arranged. There's a catch to this."

"I'm listening."

"You'll have to wear a wire."

"You didn't say all of that before, man."

"That's the conditions. From what you're telling me, it's your best bet, because it sounds as if Manuel is about to punch the clock on your ass."

"What happens if Manuel finds out I'm wired?"

"He won't. It'll be in the crack of your ass. Speaking of crack, you need to lay off that shit. You're looking real bad, man."

"How soon after this go down can I be out? Niggas will be trying to get at me."

"Same night. Don't tell anyone what's going on. You blow this operation, I'll kill you myself. So if that's all you gots to tell me, I'll be on my way. Mark your calendar for Thursday and don't let me have to come looking for you. Be at my office bright and early."

"What time?"

"5:00 AM," he said walking away. "Oh yeah. I almost forgot to tell you. Santiago was found shot to death in his apartment. You wouldn't happen to have any 411 on that, would you?" he smirked.

"Naw, man."

"I figured that."

# CHAPTER SIXTY-FIVE
## Carmello

Me and Lexi lay in my bed exhausted from fucking and sniffing all night. I'd come to discover that there was no sex like coke sex. Under the influence of such a powerful substance, you were bound to do, or try anything.

"Wanna try something new?" she asked.

"Like what?" She reached down into her purse and came up with a twenty-piece and stuck it into her pipe.

"Bitch, are you silly? I ain't smoking that shit and neither are you. Not in here anyway."

"Stop being such a punk, Mello. It's not going to kill you."

"Yo. It's bad enough I'm sniffing the shit as it is. There's no way I'm smoking it." But I guess this coke shit had me so hooked, I needed a better high. I never thought there was anything that could tie me down to its effects, but pussy and money. Just like Adam and Eve, there I was entering the garden of forbidden sin. I took a small tote and my erect dick went limp as I began to experience instant euphoria. Never was there anything so close to heaven as this. I jumped up out the bed and darted down the steps and ran around the coffee table in circles. Lexi walked down to the bottom of the steps with the pipe in hand smoking as if it was weed.

"Calm down, Mello," she said sitting on the bottom step naked.

"Come here and let me suck your dick."

My eyes were wider than they'd ever been before. My entire body was numb except for my back, which suddenly began to ache. Right then and there, I knew I was never gonna try this shit again. This feeling was crazy. After that, it was all down hill from there, like Sonic the hedgehog.

It was 8:00 PM. when my phone rang. I reached over Lexi to grab it off the night stand, only she was gone.

"H-h-hello?" I answered.

"What's the matter, baby?" Tarsha asked. My mouth was mad dry and my lips were tingling.

"Oh. Hey, ma. What's happening? You know a nigga like me is straight chilling in this muthafucka and shit."

"Mello?" she repeated, unsure if it was me speaking in such a manner.

"Yeah, boo. What the deal, yo?"

"Babe. You don't sound yourself. You alright?"

"Oh hell yeah. I just got off the phone with that crazy nigga Caine."

"Caine? Baby, stop playing around. What's going on?" I momentarily came to my senses and was able to concoct a hasty maneuver.

"Naw. I'm just kidding with you, ma. I'm kinda hung over from kicking it with the fellas earlier."

"It's only 8:00 and you're drunk?"

"It was a birthday party. I'm good now. What's going on?"

"I want you to come home, baby. I'm tired of going to the doctor by myself."

"I told you to hold it down a li'l while longer. I'm try'na get this paper straight."

"You've sent enough. Our bank account is strong now, baby. I'm still working too. You don't have to do this anymore."

"Don't tell me what I do and don't have to do, Tarsha. Let a man be a man, and handle his B.I."

"You got another week to be gone or I'll be out. You'll never see me or your son."

"Son?"

"That's right. They took a sonogram today. We're having a boy."

"I swear just a li'l longer. Then I'm out for good. I promise."

"One week."

"I got it."

"I love you, baby." I hung up the phone and looked over at the stem, coincidentally singing a Biggie tune, as I took another blast from the past. "Sky's the limit and you know that you just keep on, just keep on pressing on."

Just like any other instance in life when you're having a good time, there is always something to interrupt the pleasure principle. Red and blue lights flashed throughout my darkened room. I dropped the stem in the toilet and flushed it. Wobbling down the stairs, I fell against the front door and opened it, just as Detective Shudemall was about to ring the bell.

"Carmello Denn. We have a warrant to search your home," he said holding the paper out before me.

"A warrant for what," I responded trying to conceal my high.

"Get out the way, man. You're high on crack," he said alerting his back officers to come in.

"What the fuck, man? I ain't did shit."

"Yeah? We got several witnesses that can finger you in Santiago's building the day he was killed."

"Bullshit. I ain't never killed nobody."

"Tear this house apart until you find something," he told the leading officer. "You might as well have a seat on the couch. This could take a while. So are you ready to tell me something?"

"I can't tell you what I don't know."

"I'm sick and tired of you fucks insulting my intelligence. I'ma tell you something, Carmello. When everything finally comes to light, I'ma make sure I'm there in that courtroom when the judge sentences you to life."

"Yeah. You'd like that, wouldn't you?" I said not being able to control my fidgeting.

"Look at you. You can't even maintain your composure. You're supposed to be the former kingpin's son. Now you done fucked up and got high off your own shit. Why not just be straight with me? I can talk to the DA and get you into a real good rehab."

"I keep telling you I don't know what the fuck you are talking about!" I yelled under the pressure.

"Down boy!" he laughed, as he grabbed my shoulder. His hounds flipped everything over and still came up with nothing. So for spite, they broke up all the dishes in my kitchen.

"What's the matter, Kingpin Junior? You making all the money. You can replace all of that. Can't you?"

Then as luck would have it, my phone rang. Shude-mall snatched it off the coffee table.

"Yo?" he answered it.

"Mello?" Manuel spoke.

"No. It's the po-9. Who's this?"

"I'm sorry. I must have the wrong numero."

"No you don't. Me and your man Mello are just over here having a drink together. He was just telling me how much you two are good friends. I'm on your ass you fucking spic. You put out a contract on your own nephew? You're one fucked-up individual. You're going down. I have eyes and mouths everywhere."

"Detective, I will see you soon," Manuel calmly responded.

"Oh? Whenever. Wherever." The line disconnected and he looked back over at me.

"Tell me where he's at!" He jumped on me and began pounding me out. The officers restrained him and pulled me off to the side.

"Mike. Control yourself. The place is clean."

"You didn't find nothing?" he asked. "If there was anything here, he got rid of it before he opened the door." He looked at me with the most evil eye I ever saw in a white boy, and pointed his finger.

"It won't be long now, you fucking nigger. Just you wait and see." He stomped in my glass coffee table and my fifty-inch television screen.

"That's just to let you know I'll be back."

After they all left, my neighbors stood around outside booing them. I shut my front door and looked around at the mess they made. The phone rang again. I knew it was Manuel.

"Yeah, man?"

"Hey, bitch-nigga, this is Cash. Meet me in back of Springfield Gardens High School. I got something of yours, lover boy."

"Mello, please hurry," Lexi cried.

Being high on crack and driving just didn't mix, but I

maintained my focus. I began wondering why I was racing out 3:00 in the morning to save a bass head. Then again, at this point, who was I to talk.

I parked on 141st Avenue and Springfield Boulevard and walked to the gas station across the street from the school. I didn't see his car, or any car for that matter, except the ones drag-racing down the street through the red traffic lights. I got on the jack and chirped him.

"Yeah, bitch-nigga, I see you," he said.

"So, where you at?"

"Come around to the swimming pool entrance."

I thought about Tarsha and the baby, on my way around the building thinking, what the fuck am I doing here and why did I even came back to New York in the first place? Before, I was killing niggas with a purpose. Now, I was becoming what I never wanted to be, my father. He was a real killer. No remorse. No ethics. I was him now and disgracing the Denn name in the process, by being strung the fuck out on drugs. These things happen when you accrue so much money, you just run outta ordinary shit to do. It's like having every car you ever wanted. The next best thing to do after losing interest in driving, is to fly. I got tired of driving and decided to fly. Crack is my helicopter and hell is my landing pad.

When I got around back, the double-brown steel doors were opened. I took a deep breath and walked forward.

"Cash," I called. "Yo, Cash." I cocked the jump-off and entered. The lights around the pool came on. Then I heard another gun cock.

"Close them doors, nigga," a voice to my right spoke from the darkened corner.

"Yeah. You done fucked up now," said Cashmere coming from my left, with Lexi by his side holding a gun with a smile on her face.

"Oh. This a set up?" I said looking back to my right, trying to keep Cash and Lexi at bay. There was an unfamiliar silhouette coming towards me.

"Put that fucking gun down, nigga. You outnumbered." The voice said coming into the light. It was the dude from the bar.

"Okay, son. There he is. Can I get mines?" Cash asked.

"Yeah, you gonna get yours. But first I wanna show y'all both how you murder a bitch-ass nigga."

"Put it down," he said to me again, while Lexi and Cash moved in closer. I slowly knelt down with my hands up, and placed the gun on the wet tiled floor.

"Alright. You going to tell me what I'm dying for before you do it?" I asked the stranger.

"Yeah. Why not? Look in my face nigga and see if I look the slightest bit familiar to you?"

"Naw. I don't know any niggas that look like you."

"You try'na get smart, nigga? Huh? You try'na be smart?" he asked, slapping me across the face with the gun. I fell to the ground and quickly rose, bleeding from the eye.

"Now shut the fuck up and listen."

"I'm listening, man."

"Take a look at me and say I don't look familiar to you." I looked at him harder to see if he was old beef or somebody's whose girl I might've fucked back in the day. I just couldn't figure it out.

"Man, you sure you got the right nigga? I look like a lot of people."

"You only look like one nigga to me, and you don't know how happy I was when I heard you was back in town. You reap what you sow. Still can't figure it out? Check this tattoo," he said pulling up his shirt. "What this tat say?"

I moved a little closer.

"Keep your distance, playa. Fuck it! I'll read it for you. It says R.I.P. Todd Denn. Beloved Father." It took awhile for the shock to kick in. Then I thought back to what Uncle Todd had said before he died. That thing about how we were supposed to be his kids. Oh shit. My mother and Uncle Todd were sleeping together. But when she was pregnant back then, she'd said she miscarried at eight months.

"That name look familiar to you? We got the same mother, nigga, but you killed my father. Now I'm here to kill you."

"Oh shit, Mello. Mom dukes was a ho?" Cash said, covering his mouth with a smile.

"That's my moms too, nigga. I'm about tired of your ass." My brother raised his gun and pointed at him.

"Come on man. I was just playing."

"I'm not."

Blam! The gunshot lit up the room.

Cashmere stumbled back with one in his chest and fell into the pool. He struggled with the water for a while, then went under, shortly rising back to the surface dead.

"Told you, you was a bitch," Lexi said watching as he floated in the water. She quickly raised her gun back at me.

"So if we got the same moms, that means we brothers."

"Half-brothers, nigga. You know you destroyed my life, right? You and Caine took away the only family I had. I was only fifteen when y'all took him from me."

"He killed Mommy and my father."

"You're lying. Don't you fucking lie to me, nigga. He told me all about y'all fake-ass father."

"It wasn't true, yo. Your father stole from Santiago, then set my pops up."

"If your father hadn't stole Mommy from him, we wouldn't be here now. But we are. You ready to die, nigga?"

"No."

"Well you know what, Mello? Who gives a fuck what you ready for?"

"Come on, man. We still brothers. You saying you don't got nobody. You got me."

"I don't even know you, so it don't matter if you die."

"You going to shoot or what?" Lexi asked.

"Shut up. Just shut up."

"Listen to me, man. These is some fucked up circumstances we met upon, dawg. I never knew I had another brother. I thought everybody I had in my life was gone. Now we here. We both ain't lost out completely. I got a baby on the way and everything. You got a nephew."

"You listening to this fool? He smoking crack," Lexi said.

"We can be a family. We all we got. It can be me and you against the world. I got enough saved up so we can get out of here. We can live the good life and never do dirt again."

"You really mean that?" he asked lowering the gun.

"Yes. You my fam and I love you, Brother." We began moving closer to each other, until we embraced long and hard. He dropped the gun and he let the tears fall.

"I got a brother," he cried. "I got a brother."

"Yeah, you do." A shot went off and he was forced backwards out of my arms. He looked at me with his eyes wide open, as his body slumped to the floor.

"No!" I yelled, dropping next to him then looking back. Lexi's gun smoked, as she stood in a high-noon stance. Enoch grabbed my arm tightly gasping for life. He tried to speak, but only blood spurted out his mouth, then his grip released and his eyes closed.

"What the fuck are you doing?" I yelled grabbing both guns.

"You don't know that man. He could've been anybody."

"You just killed my brother. Now what I got?"

"Stop bitching. You didn't even know him. There's $10 thousand dollars outside the school for bringing you here. His intent was to kill you. He paid Cashmere to get you here."

"And you acted like they had you against your will."

"All part of the plan. You ready to get Manny?" she asked, walking towards the exit.

I kissed Enoch's forehead and hugged him.

"I'm sorry," I said to him.

# CHAPTER SIXTY-SIX

## *Carmello*

By morning it was all over the news about the two bodies found in the back of the school. The superintendent found them first and alerted the authorities. Shudemall was the first on the scene. Channel zero's Pulitzer prize-winning reporter, Jay Augustine, reported live on the scene.

"Sometime early this morning, a brutal shoot-out between rival gang members turned into a bloodbath on the school grounds of Springfield Garden High School. No one knows how the two men gained access inside the building, but it is believed that a student from the school left the doors unlocked hoping to catch a midnight swim in the pool. There are no leads currently, but lead Detective Mike Shudemall is in charge of the investigation. Detective, have you found anything that'll give us more insight as to what transpired last night?"

"We have no leads as of right now. But when we do, I promise the perpetrators will be convicted to the fullest extent of the law. Do you hear me? You will be caught," he stated, looking directly into the camera, as if he were talking to me.

"This is Jay Augustine for Channel Zero news, reporting live on the scene from Springfield Gardens High School in Queens. Back to you, Angela."

I clicked off the television and walked into the bathroom. Looking at myself in the mirror, I threw water on my face to bring me out of my daze. Damn I needed help. I looked real bad and this time wasn't nothing good gonna come out of this. I felt like God was punishing me for my actions. You would think a self-righteous nigga like myself, well at least the one I used to be, would be overjoyed to have a baby boy on the way. Ain't it funny how one little thing you do in life, could set you up for the ultimate downfall? Even when you think you're doing what's best, it's still all bullshit. It seems like a set-up for us to be poor, just to make an honest living. We're brought up our entire life believing we can be whatever we want to be when we grow up. Yeah. We can be whatever we want to be, as long as they let us. They ain't happy unless we serving them their food or serving a lifetime sentence.

Half of us can't even read a fucking sentence, so how do we grow up and become anything we want? We don't. We become what they want: drug dealers, pimps, drug addicts, homeless vagrants, killers, murderers, casualties, statistics, examples, problematic socialites, interested more in dressing hood than addressing the conditioning of the hood by primary candidates of the congressional Ku Klux Klan. Instead of being part of the solution, I was definitely a part of the problem. Fuck it. I'ma keep it real with myself. I been the fucking problem. It's been a long time coming but I know a change is gonna come, because at the end of the day, I'm still Carmello.

For the next couple of days nothing in the street could move without the dicks running up on something. Anybody that sneezed wrong was harassed, then searched. Shudemall was steady trying to find out who killed Enoch and Cashmere, and I was forced to shut shit down indefinitely. Word on the wire was that I was hanging by a string with a bell, meaning I was the hottest thing out since three bitches with gonorrhea. Shudemall was steady trying to find a way to pin the murders on me, along with Santiago's.

Just when I thought things couldn't any worse, guess what? They did!

# CHAPTER SIXTY-SEVEN

## Shudemall

"This fucking guy comes back into town, and bodies start dropping everywhere. He's been gone for two fucking months for Christ's sake. It was your responsibility to keep an eye on this guy, Mike!" Shudemall's superior yelled at him. "Why isn't this guy on camera doing anything?"

"What do you think I've been doing? Scratching my balls, Chief? Him and that fucking Manuel are becoming fucking untouchable. Nobody is talking, and no one is seeing shit. How does a man go from a hated snitch, to the big man on campus after being off the scene for two years?"

"It's Santiago and Carmello Sr. all over again," said the chief. "This shit must end. I want two guys at his house twenty-four hours a day. He has got to fuck up somewhere along the way. I lost a lot of good agents behind this Carmello bullshit."

"You have to give it to them though, Chief. Those muthafuckas had a long run. And if Carmello Sr. would've kept paying, everybody would still be alive. But he wanted to leave. And fucking Carlos. That was such a lovely set up to make Santiago turn on him."

"None of this is going the way we planned anymore. I never expected to lose Kilaneega and Gurthy. It's all getting out of hand now. I think it's really time to bring Manuel and Carmello down. It was easier using Cashmere as our donut boy. Now he's dead. We're losing money. I can't prove it, but I just know that Carmello is at the bottom of this. He must've had some idea Cashmere was going to start talking."

"Why wouldn't you think Manuel had him killed?" Shudemall asked.

"Too sloppy. It wasn't a planned hit. It was a sporadic and reflexive reaction. The way I figure, Carmello was trying to pump information out of Cashmere and he got scared, so scared that he drew a weapon, but Carmello just happened to be quicker on the draw."

"And what about the other guy?"

"That I don't know. He has no criminal background. Just the average joe associating with the wrong crowd. Poor schmuck."

"At the end of the day, I want to see Carmello go down. He is his father's son and shouldn't be allowed to get away with murder. These fucking niggers and foreigners always take more than what they're given. It stops now."

"What do you have in mind?"

"Before he feels like his back is against the wall, he will make a deal with somebody to cover his ass. He'll snitch on Manuel. So I think I'll pay him a visit and sway him into believing that Carmello is fucking with the CIA. After Manuel takes care of him, we'll take care of Manuel."

"It must look clean, Mike. It must look clean," the chief said, kicking his feet up on his desk, lighting a cigar.

# CHAPTER SIXTY-EIGHT

## *Carmello*

"Carmello, you are beginning to disappoint me," Manuel said on the flight to Miami in his private jet. He had a home out there and felt obligated to drag me along on a little vacation. I really felt like I was going backwards. This was damn-near where all of my troubles began in the first place.

"Look, man. If you're talking about my so-called drug addiction, I already told you it's under control now. I'm good."

"You're good? I do not think so. No one stops smoking crack on a whim."

"It's not that serious, man. I can handle it."

"The policia have been a burden to me ever since you joined forces with me. Is there anything you'd like to say?"

"Say like what? You trying to say something, just say it."

"I've been hearing things that do not sit very well with me."

"Oh yeah? Like what, Manny?"

"What is your relation to Detective Shudemall?"

"Back to that again? It's all bullshit and politics. Whatever he's telling you is his attempt to cause confusion. You know this game. You know what the beast is all about. We both been seeing that paper. I'm a big reason why you are doing these big thangs."

"Your problem is, you think the world is in your hands. You once again, just like with Santiago, have forgotten how you gained what you have."

"I ain't forgot shit. But both y'all muthafuckas think that just because you put a nigga on, means you can talk to me any way you want. And I just ain't having it. I'm a fucking man just like you. Nobody gonna disrespect me."

"You've changed so much from the time we've first met. Your caliber. Your vocabulary. Your spirit. The drive you once possessed has been murdered by your greed and arrogance." Manny pulled out his personal stash of soda and took a quick hit. He rubbed his nose and sneezed.

"Furthermore, I did not lend you Lexi to keep fucking her as if she belongs to you. She is mine. From this day forth, I'd advise you to no longer associate with her. This is not a request."

Here I was on a private jet listening to this fool say all kinda crazy shit, then he brings the bitch into it. This shit was starting to play out like something out of an urban fiction book.

# CHAPTER SIXTY-NINE

## *Carmello*

"I'm leaving you, Carmello. This is it. I gave you op-portunity after opportunity to come back home. You been saying you'd be home next week, every week, for the past four months. Apparently you are not inter-ested in being a father to your child. Your shit is back in front of your house on the porch. Whenever you do get back, don't bother calling or coming to my house. I'll be long gone. I won't have my son growing up knowing his daddy is a drug-dealer, a murderer, or whatever it is you do to make your money," Tarsha said on my voicemail.

It didn't matter though. It probably was for the best. I didn't need my son seeing me all fucked up. I liked this life now. I wasn't gonna change. Nothing mattered to me anymore but the high. I couldn't shake the shit. I guess that old saying was true, once you smoke crack, you never go back. To Cali or sanity. How fucking ironic. So fucking ironic. I took a flight out of Miami back to Cali-fornia the next night without Manuel's knowledge.

It was 11:00 PM and pouring rain, when I pounded on her front door. Despite what she told me, I loved her and she was having my baby. Regardless of what I'd said earlier, they were all I had left. I just couldn't lose my very last bit of sanity. I looked through the window of the darkened home until a light finally came on. Then a figure walked down the stairs.

"Who is it?" Tarsha asked through the closed door.

"Baby, it's Mello. Can we talk?"

"What do you want, Mello. I told you not to come here anymore. I'm going to call the police."

"Come on, Tarsha. Let me just talk to you for a minute."

"There's nothing we have to discuss. You had your chance, and that's it."

"Come on, Tarsha. You know I was gone for so long for a reason. It was for us."

"Mello, that's bullshit. You was going to school. You was getting it together. How'd you end up doing the same shit you was doing that got you shot in the first place? That's not the kind of life I want for my child."

"Why you keep saying your child? He's my child too."

"Not anymore. Please leave."

"Tarsha, I'm not playing with you. You better open this door."

"I'm calling the police now."

"Call them muthafuckas," I said kicking the door.

"Hello? Police? My ex-boyfriend is outside my door, trying to kick it in, and will not leave. I'm five months pregnant and scared," I heard her say through the door, over the phone.

"Fuck them!" I said finally kicking the door open.

Tarsha dropped the phone, after I kicked it open, and fell down on the first step leading upstairs. I picked up the phone.

"Hello? Hello? Is everything alright ma'am?" the operator said.

"Everything is fine, operator," I said. "My girlfriend

and I are just having a small disagreement. We're fine now."

I put my fingers to my lips and quietly shushed Tarsha. She backed up to the second step.

"Are you sure, sir?"

"Everything is fine."

"Okay, sir. Have a good evening," she said before disconnecting the call.

"You got some kind of nerve, Tarsha," I said slamming the door. "I ain't never did nothing to you, but shell out doe and time. Then when I'm gone just for a hot second, you wanna start tripping?"

"Gone for a hot second? You've been gone a little longer than that."

"Tarsha, I was broke as shit, man. I was sitting on top of some real bullshit. I'm not used to struggling like that. Then you come into my life and I'm rich again. Just not rich enough to buy you everything you always wanted."

"It was never about the money with me. I have my own. You got back into what you did because you can't seem to shake the hustle. I can't live like that."

"You don't like living like a queen?"

"Yes, I do, but not if I have to live like a queen in fear. I couldn't live with the fact of you getting killed or going to jail for life, trying to provide me with materialistic shit. I couldn't and I'm not."

"I'm almost thirty years old, Tarsha. Where can I work at this point in my life? Where I can afford to take care of a wife and a child?"

"A wife?"

"Yeah. A wife. I love you like that. You're all I got, yo. I need you in my life."

"Oh. You need me?"

"You don't feel the same?"

"I love you, Mello. I really do, but if you can't walk away from the life right here, right now, then we're finished. I never spent any of the money you sent me. I put it away in an account for you. So now you have a brand new start. There's over $150 thousand in it."

"I don't want it. It's for you and the baby."

"So what's it going to be? The streets, or us?" she asked holding her stomach.

"You already know the answer to that."

"I need to hear you say it. Not just to me, but to your son too."

"I need to finish tying up these loose ends back in New York. All I need is two days and I'll never leave your side again."

"What loose ends? What reason do you have to go back? You're already here. Just stay."

"You know I can't just walk away like that. I don't need anybody coming out here looking for me again, especially now," I said sitting next to her, putting my hand on her stomach.

"When do you have to leave?"

Just as I was about to answer, my cell rang.

"Hello?"

"Carmello. Are you trying to skip out on me?" Manuel asked.

"I had to fly out and handle some business."

"Your business is here. This does not look good on your part."

"I know, but it was important. I'll be landing at JFK sometime tomorrow."

"What's important, is your business here. I'll see you at my place by 2:00 PM tomorrow afternoon."

"I have to go," I said looking at her.

"Please just stay the night," she pleaded hugging me.

# CHAPTER SEVENTY

## *Carmello*

I landed at JFK airport around 12:15 in the afternoon. Lexi was there to pick me up as soon as I exited the lobby doors.

"Welcome home, playa," she smiled from the driver's seat.

"What's up? I guess Manuel sent you?"

"I wasn't leaving until you walked through those doors. Manuel has a huge shipment coming in. There's a lot of money involved. Today is the day."

"The day for what?"

"The day Manuel is no more. This is what we've been waiting for." A feeling in my gut told me that today was also the day Manuel was going to kill me. If not that, then something. He didn't tell me anything about a shipment. Was Lexi just talking to stall for time?

She dropped me off at my house and said she'd call in about two hours. My phone rang off the chain with call after call from Manuel. I didn't answer it. As darkness crawled over the evening sky, I turned off all the lights in my house. Finally around 8:00 PM, an unfamiliar number appeared on the screen of my phone. I pushed the answer button, but never responded.

"Carmello. I know you're there. This is Shudemall. You're going down. We have video surveillance from Santiago's apartment. You killed him and that makes you a fucking liar. This time, you won't beat the rap, but I might be able to make this all go away if you just come in and talk to me. Better yet, meet me back at the park where we first spoke. You have my word, there'll be no tricks or strings attached."

"What time?" I finally spoke.

"Right now."

I walked to my window and pulled the blinds down to look out over the parking lot. There was no sight of any cars. The light posts shined exceptionally bright. I ran out the condo and jumped into my car. I left behind a trail of exhaust, as I peeled out the parking lot. When I got to the park, Shudemall was sitting on the park bench. As I approached, he stood up with his hand extended. I kept my hands in my pockets.

"My man, Carmello. Big time. What's up?"

"What you want from me, man?"

"You know what I want. Manuel. I hear there's a big shipment coming in tonight. My superior has the tape of you killing Santiago. You tell me everything I want to know, and the tape disappears."

"I can't do that."

"Oh yeah? You can't do that, huh? Don't you know if you get locked up what'll happen to you? Manuel has a lot of friends. Miguel, his brother, has even more. So whether you're locked up or out on the streets, your time is coming. Now you can either take your chances with me, or you can take your chances with them. You make the choice." He had a point. I didn't want to be a snitch again, but what was I supposed to do? I made a promise to Tarsha to leave this alone. This could be my way out and if I told him what he wanted to know, it would give me enough time to bounce and move Tarsha out of California. He'd never find us. Yeah right. People like him always had ways of finding whoever they wanted to. Then again? There was always plan B. Lexi's plan.

"How do you know about this so-called big shipment?"

"Lexington Maxwell."

"Who?"

"You know her as Lexi. She fears for her life. She's been giving us little bits here and there. In return, we free her from her predicament."

"So Lexi is a snitch?"

"I prefer informant."

"Oh. That's better. Informant is so different than snitch."

"It's better to be alive than dead, man. Hey. You put yourself in this shit hole, Carmello. If you don't wanna be around for the birth of your son, then I can make the call now and you'll be picked up. You'll get life in prison, but you probably won't serve the full sentence because the animals in there won't let you survive. Nobody likes a snitch."

"You're a real bastard, you know that?"

"Comes with the job. You should know about that, snitch, I mean informer."

In order to get back home to Tarsha I had to do what I had to do. I called Lexi.

"Lexi, I'm ready to do this."

"I'm at his house now. He's in the shower. Where have you been? He's been calling you all day. You can't play games with him like this."

"Before we do this, we need to talk" I said.

"Can't it wait until after?"

"There may not be time. We need to talk before we do this."

"So talk."

"Not over the phone."

"What's this about, Mello? You backing out on me?"

"Should I have a reason to?"

"Look. I don't have time for the Q and A routine. There is no way Manuel's going to let me leave here while we're waiting on that pick up. So just say what you have to say to me now, because there won't be any time when you get here."

"You fucking with the feds, bitch?"

"What? No. Who told you that?"

"That's why you want to kill Manuel so bad. You want to put it all on me. Yeah that's right. Shudemall told me everything."

"Carmello, you don't understand. Trust me. Shudemall is dirty."

"I understand that. What I don't understand is you. What's your angle in all this?"

"I can't talk over the phone. I'll see what I can do to get away for a minute, but you must be with me when I return."

"I'm already about ten minutes away. I'll be parked at the 7-11 across the street from the Saudi gas station."

"I'm leaving the house right now."

We both pulled into the 7-11 parking lot at the same time. I got inside her car and turned the music down.

"Alright. So what's up?" she said.

"You know what, Lexington?" She spun her head around quickly and faced me.

"Figured that'd get your attention Lexington Maxwell. You been talking to me about bumping off this faggot ass Manuel, and all this time you fucking with the police?"

"There's a lot you don't understand, Carmello."

"You keep saying that, so make me fucking understand."

"I can't."

"Then tell me why I shouldn't blast your muthafucking ass, right now?" I asked putting my hand on the handle of my gun.

"Playtime is over. I suggest you let that piece rest where it sits," she said without a sign of worry on her face.

"You a real bold bitch for somebody who, not too long ago, popped my brother to death."

"I felt threatened. He had both guns drawn. I didn't know what he was going to do."

"What in the fuck are you talking about? You stood right there after he dropped his shit and shot anyway."

"This is much, much bigger than you. In this game there's going to be casualties of war. Yes, it is unfortunate your brother had to die, but he placed himself in the middle of a situation that is on its way to spilling over."

"You better do better than that."

This time I cocked the gun and put it to her temple.

"Start driving, Lexi. If you even blink wrong, I swear to God, I'll kill you. I don't need your ass to handle Manuel." She reversed out the parking lot keeping an eye on me and the oncoming road before us.

"Where do you want me to drive?" she asked.

"Just out the light."

She drove to the empty parking lot of abandoned warehouses and kept her hands on the steering wheel.

"Spill it, Lexi. I don't have time for no bullshit no more," I threatened, tapping her in the side of the head with the gun.

"Okay, damn it. Okay. Open my purse."

"Keep your fucking hands on that steering wheel," I

growled. "What am I supposed to be looking for in here?"

"You'll know when you see it, smart guy." Expecting to come up with drugs I came up on what else? Some more of my famous bad luck. Lexi a.k.a Lexington Maxwell was Internal Affairs.

"Aww shit, not again. Another fucking cop? Fuck it. I give up. I'm tired of this shit," I said tossing my gun in her lap.

"Uh-uh, playa. Too late for all of that now. You're going to help me bring down Shudemall. We've been on his trail for years. He's been extorting money from the streets ever since the days of his former partner Kilaneega."

"Yo. I'm done. I don't want to hear shit. It's a fucking wrap. Y'all shit is mad deep. Every aspect of the government. Call who you gots to call. Take my black ass in."

"Oh. We'll do more than that. While you're in jail fighting for your life, your son will be born in jail along with his mother. All of that money you've been sending her is drug money. Marked money."

I looked at her like, damn. The government doesn't miss a note.

"Yeah, the money you've been sending her all this time, has she reported it in her taxes? Where does almost $200,000 just appear out of nowhere? In a dummy account at that. She's only making $30,000 a year. That doesn't amount to nearly that in five months. And for the record Enoch wasn't your brother. He was an informant of ours that we used awhile back, and his mouth started running a bit too much, so we sent him in as a decoy to coax you into doing our bidding."

"What? So you killed him?"

"Like I told you, this is bigger than you'll ever understand. If you help us out with this, help us take Shude-mall and Manuel together, you'll never be bothered by anyone ever again. You can go on resuming your normal life. All the monies you've sent over to Tarsha can stay in the account."

"How do I know I can trust you?"

"What choice do you have? Make no mistake about it, Manuel does plan on killing you after the transactions have materialized. So what are you going to do?"

"So what was all this talk about killing Manuel?"

"It would've bought Shudemall and his department closer to the front line. But now things have changed. He's trying to pull out with one big bust. He wants to use you as the scapegoat."

"And you?"

"I'm just doing my job."

"You smoked with me and fucked."

"It's part of my job description. Do whatever it takes to bring down the perp. You're small fish. Shudemall's the shark. Manuel is the whale. Ready to go fish?"

# CHAPTER SEVENTY-ONE

## Carmello

My body was aching for a blast of rock. I ain't never had a hunger like this in my entire life. But I knew I had to be on point later tonight. I'd finally spoken to Manuel and he wanted me to meet him at the pier in Jersey. There'd be a ship docking in around midnight. Manuel had men sporadically spread out around the shipping area, securely holding it down, in the event of an unexpected bust. I flashed my lights twice to alert everyone I was here. Two men with automatic sub weapons escorted me to a docking house two miles from the site. Manuel was inside with Lexi, both of them sniffing their way into oblivion. Something didn't feel right. Security monitors sat across the long wooden table with an arsenal of weapons.

"Ahh, Carmello. Sit. Sit," he said removing his sunglasses. "Have you gotten it all out of your system yet?"

"What's that, Manny?"

"Running away."

"I didn't run away. I had a personal matter I needed to handle."

"So I take it all is well now? After all, you have returned. Not promptly, but returned nevertheless."

"Everything is cool."

"Good. As I've said on the plane, I think our business relationship after tonight should be dissolved. Do you have any qualms with that?"

"None."

"Very well."

"I'm going to take a piss. I'll be right back," I said walking out to the back.

"Carmello, leave your phone please. I wouldn't want anyone hearing it ring," he said.

"Who's gonna hear it ring this far out?"

"Maybe you're expecting an important call from a friend?" he curiously suggested. I pulled my phone out my back pocket and placed it in front of him.

"That is much better. I cannot afford to have such an opportunity such as this be thwarted by coincidence or neglect. What is the matter, Mello. You do not greet Lexi anymore?" I gave her a nod and moved on to the back. I pulled the battery from my phone out my pocket, and wiped perspiration from my forehead. I checked the wire in my sock to make sure it was now transmitting, then took my piss into the water.

While ships periodically passed one another, I stood and watched, pondering how I was going to live out the rest of my life married with children. It'd be nice to sit on the couch after a hard day's work with my hand stuffed down the front of my pants. Maybe a lazy dog. Yeah. I was going to love the simple life. Who was I kidding? I didn't know if I could ever get used to living like a homebody, but whatever Tarsha wanted, she was going to get.

"Carmello, it's going down," Lexi said out the window. The guards all lined up in place and I ran inside to

watch the monitors, along with Manuel. I didn't see anything.

"Where is it?" I asked.

All I saw next was Lexi's neck snap back, with a clear
plastic bag over it. I was next. We both struggled while
our bodies were flung around the room until we fell on
our faces. A hole was poked in the plastic so I could
breathe. Lexi wasn't as fortunate. Both our hands were
tied behind our backs, as we struggled for air. Lexi
squirmed and kicked, struggling to breathe until a hole
was poked in hers. We were pulled to our feet by his men
and placed back to back against the base-pole between
the ceiling and the floor. The heat from it burned our
backs.

"Manuel, man. What the fuck is this?" I yelled breath-
lessly.

"You think I am a fool?"

"What you talking about?"

"Special Agent Loretta Cuttley can explain it to you
much better. Can't you?" he said grabbing her chin. "I
have eyes and ears everywhere."

"Wait a minute, Manuel. Give me a second to explain,"
Lexi pleaded.

"No! You are in violation of a Decosta. It is now time to
die."

"When are they to come?" he asked.

"When is who to come? What are you talking about?"

"You disappoint me, Loretta Cuttley. All the places
and things I've shown you. I am sure they will miss you
at the office. Juan, find the wire," he commanded. His
goon, Juan, ripped her blouse off, then her skirt. She
screamed and was quieted by a stunning slap to the
mouth. Standing just in her panties, she sniffled.

"How do you like her body, Juan?" Manuel asked.

"Si," he replied grinning.

"Do with her as you will," Manuel granted him.

"No. Don't do this. Manuel, no," she begged.

I could feel her struggling to avoid Juan's forceful attempt to penetrate her center, as I heard her panties torn from her waist.

"Do you see how they try to destroy me, Carmello? They send pretty women to me and have them play a role like some kind of movie. I always hated going to the movies as a bambino, and I do not care for them as a man."

Where the hell was Shudemall? I was damn-near pissing my pants. It was one thing knowing you were going to die, but not seeing it coming was even worse. Shit. Was this transmitter even working?

"Manuel. Two helicopters I see," said another goon, running inside from off the deck.

"Get the money. We must leave. Burn this down," he yelled.

The smell of gasoline raped my nostrils and momentarily made me dizzy.

"It has been my pleasure knowing you," Manuel said, slapping the side of my face.

The back door to the small deck-house was flung open and feet scattered.

"FBI" a familiar voice shouted. The roaring of the helicopters became louder, and the house began to shake. Warring machine guns overrode the foghorns sounding off from the ships.

"Get on the fucking floor!" Shudemall shouted to Manuel, Juan, and the three other men inside. Shudemall pulled the bag off my head, then Lexi's. He put his jacket around her naked body, and untied both our hands.

"Señor Shudemall, it is good to see you," Manuel said, face-down on the floor.

"Didn't I tell you I would catch you sooner or later?"

"You have nothing."

"Where's the money?" he asked stepping on Manuel's neck.

Red and blue lights flashed outside, accompanied by ear piercing sirens, running feet, and physical, combative struggling.

"Get your hands over your heads!" Shudemall yelled to me and Lexi.

A flash grenade broke through the window and temporarily disoriented everyone's vision.

"D.E.A.!" another commanding voice yelled, running through the front door with a squad of agents behind him, weapons drawn.

"FBI!" Shudemall yelled, holding up the badge hanging around his neck, while using his other hand to shield his eyes.

"Internal Affairs," another commanding voice shouted, barging through the back door, with a group of twelve men.

"It's over Shudemall," Lexi said. "Internal Affairs." The leading officer of I.A. passed her identification to her.

"No," Shudemall said.

"We have everything we need to put you away for a long time," she said.

"What proof?" Shudemall asked.

"Carmello," she said as she looked at me.

# CHAPTER SEVENTY-TWO

## *Carmello*

I couldn't believe it was finally all over. And when I say finally over, I meant it. I never thought it would be a government official that saved my life. But Lexington, I mean, Special Agent Loretta Cuttley, did just that. She also kept her promise and never snitched about the money I'd been sending to Tarsha in the dummy account.

Shudemall was sentenced to twenty-five years. There never was a video-tape of me killing Santiago, and Manuel's shipment never came, but he was charged with distribution.

Manuel was deported back to Colombia to serve the rest of his natural life in prison.

When I got back out to California, I got myself admitted into a twelve-step drug rehabilitation program. My first child, my son, Saundese was born July 25th at 1:23 AM. Tarsha and I bought a home in the Bay Area and I got myself back into school. A year later, we married and had twin girls, China and Cierra.

# EPILOGUE

*Five Years Later*

I graduated from college with a Masters in Child Psychology, and started up a Big Brother's club in the hood. I didn't want to see another child go through the life I experienced. I wanted them to know there was more to life than just the hustle, more to life than just a quick dollar. Sometimes children needed to see other avenues, than just taking the street life. I was fortunate enough to escape its grasp and come out unscathed, finally.

Now my children will learn, through me, what it is to embrace your family while you have them, and to lead by example, not influence. Every so often we fly out to New York and visit my family's gravesites.

We were all in the family room watching a movie, when the doorbell rang.

"I'll get it," Saundese, now five, said running to the door.

"Saundese! Get away from that door, I'll get it, baby. Can you keep an eye on the girls. I'll get it," Tarsha said.

"Who is it?" I heard Saundese say.

"Get away from that door, boy," Tarsha smiled, as she walked to the door.

"Fed-Ex," the deliveryman said, through the screen door.

"You expecting something, babe?" Tarsha asked, looking back half-way to the door.

"Naw. I didn't order anything."

"Get away from that door, baby," Tarsha said, running to the door with me right behind her. Saundese was already pushing the door open, when the deliveryman pulled the gun out of the boxed package. He quickly looked at us and smiled, then pointed the gun at my son.

"No, wait!" I yelled.